I've travelled the world twice over,
Met the famous: saints and sinners,
Poets and artists, kings and queens,
Old stars and hopeful beginners,
I've been where no-one's been before,
Learned secrets from writers and cooks
All with one library ticket
To the wonderful world of books.

© Janice James.

The wisdom of the ages
Is there for you and me,
The wisdom of the ages,
In your local library

There's large print books
And talking books,
For those who cannot see,
The wisdom of the ages,
It's fantastic, and it's free.

Written by Sam Wood, aged 92

A BURIAL IN PORTUGAL

When word reaches the Queen's and Lord Treasurer's Remembrancer in Edinburgh that Francis Preston has been found dead in the ruins of an old Moorish fort in Portugal, Jonathan Gaunt is sent to the funeral. Preston had fallen foul of the Remembrancer's office when he'd located a rich hoard of Treasure Trove in Scotland, and Gaunt's orders are to uncover the secret of Preston's find. With Preston's death shaping like murder, and other brutal deaths quickly following, Jonathan Gaunt's role soon switches from hunter to hunted . . .

Books by Bill Knox
Published by The House of Ulverscroft:

SEAFIRE
CHILDREN OF THE MIST
THE KLONDYKER
STORMTIDE
THE DEEP FALL
TO KILL A WITCH
HELLSPOUT
DEATH DEPARTMENT
RALLY TO KILL
WHITEWATER
THE TASTE OF PROOF
DEADLINE FOR A DREAM
BOMBSHIP
A KILLING IN ANTIQUES
THE HANGING TREE
WAVECREST
THE CROSSFIRE KILLINGS
THE COCKATOO CRIME
DEAD MAN'S MOORING
THE INTERFACE MAN
LEAVE IT TO THE HANGMAN
DEVILWEED

BILL KNOX

◆

A BURIAL IN PORTUGAL

Complete and Unabridged

ULVERSCROFT
Leicester

First published in Great Britain

Originally published under name of
'Robert MacLeod'

First Large Print Edition
published 1997

British Library CIP Data

Knox, Bill, *1928 –*
   A burial in Portugal.—Large print ed.—
Ulverscroft large print series: mystery
1. English fiction—20th century
2. Large type books
I. Title II. MacLeod, Robert, *1928 –*
823.9'14 [F]

ISBN 0–7089–3704–7

Published by
F. A. Thorpe (Publishing) Ltd.
Anstey, Leicestershire
Set by Words & Graphics Ltd.
Anstey, Leicestershire
Printed and bound in Great Britain by
T. J. Press (Padstow) Ltd., Padstow, Cornwall

This book is printed on acid-free paper

For Grace and Ross

QUEEN'S AND LORD TREASURER'S REMEMBRANCER

H.M. Exchequer Office

'Para. 35. With regard to Treasure Trove, articles of antiquarian or archaeological interest are claimed on behalf of the Crown and rewards are made to the finders after consultation with the Keeper of the National Museum of Antiquities of Scotland.'

1

EARLY spring had returned colour again to Edinburgh after the long Scottish winter. It burst triumphantly from the thousands of daffodils and crocuses in Princes Street Gardens, danced and rippled on the dresses of girls free after months in fur boots and sheepskin jackets — even showed in the way warm sunlight caught and played with the drab stonework of the Sir Walter Scott Monument, that high, ridiculous neo-Gothic tracery on the Scottish capital's skyline.

But it would be raining again by lunch, decided Henry Falconer. A big, heavy-faced man, senior administrative assistant to the Queen's and Lord Treasurer's Remembrancer, he flopped down on one of the wooden benches spaced along the gardens and ignored the flowers around. The sun was hurting his eyes, his head wouldn't stop throbbing, and he damned those extra drinks he'd had

1

at the previous night's Civil Service Golf Club dinner.

"You said you wanted to walk, Henry," murmured Jonathan Gaunt, fighting down a grin and stopping beside him. "Feeling tired?"

"No." Falconer scowled around at the rest of the world, at that moment mainly a mini-skirted blonde walking a large, bored Labrador dog on a lead. Escaping from his office in the Exchequer Building had seemed a good idea, at the time, but now he wasn't sure. "Sit down, man. I also said we'd talk."

Gaunt obeyed, watching the girl and the dog as they came nearer. The girl had the kind of legs he liked, long, slim, and firmly muscled all the way up to the thigh.

"Would it be too much trouble to ask you to listen?" asked Falconer acidly, his annoyance plain.

"Sorry." Gaunt reluctantly switched his attention. "What's the problem?"

"Yours — and you'll need a black tie," said Falconer with grim satisfaction. "You're going to a funeral tomorrow."

"I am?" Gaunt raised a mildly surprised

eyebrow. "Anyone I know?"

"No, but someone we've been interested in." Falconer paused and shrugged. "This is the Remembrancer's idea, not mine, and it happens no one else is free to go. You'll need . . . "

Gaunt held up a hand to stop him and let the grin slide openly across his wide mouth. "A black tie — you told me, Henry. That must have been one hell of a party last night."

"It was." Falconer winced at the reminder but went on doggedly. "But I intended to say you'll need your passport. The funeral is in Portugal."

"Portugal?" Gaunt stared at him.

It brought Falconer a little glow of pleasure. From his viewpoint, catching the younger man off guard was something which didn't happen often enough.

"Portugal," he agreed. "That's on the left-hand side of Spain, as I recall."

"Thanks, Henry," said Gaunt wryly, recovering. "All right, what makes it matter so much we can't just wire a wreath?"

Falconer looked at him, feeling a familiar irritation gathering. From outlook onward,

3

Jonathan Gaunt just didn't blend with the accepted qualities of an external auditor in the Remembrancer's Office.

Gaunt was in his early thirties, tall and with a compact build. A raw-boned face, faintly freckled, went with moody grey-green eyes and fair hair which always seemed untidy and too long. Even his clothes were annoyingly wrong for the job, decided Falconer. A lightweight tweed sports suit worn with a blue shirt and a knitted tie in a darker blue, plus moccasin style shoes, didn't add up to Government service wear.

"You do have a black tie, I presume?" asked Falconer wearily.

"Somewhere." The girl with the dog went past. Gaunt made a clicking noise at the dog, who ignored him, and smiled at the girl, who appeared more interested. He waited till they'd gone a few yards then turned to Falconer again. "Well? What's it all about?"

Falconer shrugged. "The — ah — deceased is a man named Francis Preston." He saw the name didn't register, grimaced slightly and went on. "Preston mattered to us because he found

4

something. Found it, then walked away and left it there."

Puzzled, Gaunt stared at him. "If you're trying out some new kind of riddle . . . " he began threateningly.

"I'm not." Falconer sounded bitter, looked down with a sigh, and scraped a foot along the ground. "Preston had us over the proverbial barrel. Now he's dead, the Remembrancer wants you to negotiate a reward of up to £50,000 to anyone who can tell us what he wouldn't."

"Fifty thousand!" Gaunt sat bolt upright on the bench, his lips shaping a startled whistle. "For what?"

"Treasure Trove. The file is on my desk." Falconer looked around at the flowers and shook his head uneasily, a man who needed more familiar surroundings when it came to business. "Maybe we should go back there."

"We'd better," agreed Gaunt fervently.

On the way, they stopped in a Princes Street shop while Gaunt bought a new black tie. Francis Preston already sounded as if he deserved it.

* * *

The Queen's and Lord Treasurer's Remembrancer occupies part of the Exchequer Building in Edinburgh's George Street. Henry Falconer's office was on the second floor and he settled into his chair with considerable relief.

"What do you know about Treasure Trove?" he demanded with a new assurance.

"From a legal viewpoint?" Jonathan Gaunt scrubbed a hand along his chin. "The usual definition is anything of value found hidden for which no owner can be discovered. *Ultimus Haeres* section usually handle it."

Falconer nodded. "Any man-made items are presumed to have once had an owner. But in his absence they belong directly to the crown, not to the finder. The law is fairly similar in most countries — the only difference is whether the finder gets a specific share of the value or whether he simply gets a reward."

He stopped as there was a knock on the door. His secretary, a well-built

6

brunette with a distant air, brought in two mugs of coffee. The one she placed before Falconer was black and she gave him a cold glance of disapproval then left without a word.

"Damn the woman," muttered Falconer, using a Government issue pencil to stir his brew. "What she needs . . . " he stopped and sighed.

"The word is anyone who tries that with her gets frostbite." Gaunt sipped his mug then set it down. "She's your problem, Henry. What about mine? I thought we had a clear routine for Treasure Trove claims?"

"We have — for the regular variety." Falconer took a long, thankful gulp of his coffee and dabbed his lips with a handkerchief. "Maybe a bulldozer digs up a chest of old coins, or a child playing in some ruin comes out clutching a bag of gold. We once had a farmer who had a cow fall down a hole — when he got it out, he discovered a Bronze Age hoard of vital archaeological importance."

"I could use a cow like that," mused Gaunt.

Falconer ignored him. "Large or small,

7

all finds of value must be surrendered. Then the Remembrancer puts a committee of experts to work. They decide the probable open market value and pay a reward to the finder."

"Who goes away happily?"

"Not always," admitted Falconer. "But the law is specific. Find something and keep it and you commit a criminal offence. The penalties are severe." He stopped and swirled his coffee, frowning. "But find something, cover it up again, walk away and refuse to talk about it — that's not an offence."

Suddenly, Gaunt began to understand. "Francis Preston?"

"Preston," agreed Falconer grimly. "He was a fairly well-known amateur archaeologist, among other things. About a year ago he contacted the Remembrancer direct and said he'd made an important find somewhere on the northwest coast. From the description he gave, it amounted to a major find of early Christian church plate — probably hidden just before a Viking raid, with the people who concealed it massacred soon afterwards."

"Uncomplicated people, the Vikings,"

murmured Gaunt. "But Preston found the stuff — then tried to do a deal?"

Falconer nodded. "Money didn't particularly interest him. But he wanted the final say on what happened to the church plate. His main demand was that most of it should be gifted to some Scottish university for all time as the Preston Collection."

"Reasonable enough, Henry — he found the stuff."

"But the system doesn't work that way," snapped Falconer and scowled. "It was explained to him, but . . ."

"But he told the Remembrancer to get stuffed?"

Falconer nodded. "Then walked out. He hadn't removed the plate from where he found it so we couldn't touch him. And though we had certain people try, we couldn't find a single lead to where he might have been." Still scowling, Falconer stopped, shoved a thick manilla file across the desk towards Gaunt, and glanced at a slip of paper. "So you're booked on a flight which gets you to Lisbon early tomorrow afternoon. The funeral is at four p.m.

and afterwards . . . "

"Use tact, discretion, and wave all that money around," nodded Gaunt. "Henry, suppose I tell you I'd have been on Preston's side?"

"I'm not interested in any parade of your morality or conscience," said Falconer wearily. "Just find where that damned stuff is. It may take you a few days, but we'll switch any work you've got at the moment onto someone else."

Gaunt grimaced. "That leaves a few personal problems . . . "

"We all have those," said Falconer bleakly, uninterested. "You'll see from the file that Preston died rather oddly. He was on some archaeological project on the Portugese coast when a trench collapsed on him. He was dead when they dug him out."

"When?"

"Two days ago. Word only got to us this morning. We have to gamble that those people closest to him, people who might know, will be there at the funeral. What matters is we're offering £50,000 — if the plate is what he claimed."

Gaunt picked up the file and rose.

"Thanks," he said sardonically. "Anything else?"

"A small warning." Falconer nursed his coffee mug between both hands. "As I recall it, there's a casino in Estoril, just along the coast. Just remember your expenses only cover legitimate claims."

"And if I win?"

"In that unlikely event — " Falconer's face thawed into the makings of a hopeful smile " — you might remember less fortunate colleagues who are tied to their desks by responsibility. The wine of the country . . . "

"I'll remember," promised Gaunt.

"Good. And — ah — you can charge that black tie to the Department, of course," said Falconer expansively.

"I'll try to remember that too," said Gaunt, keeping a straight face as he went out.

Once the door had closed Henry Falconer sighed, fumbled a couple of aspirins from his waistcoat pocket, and swallowed them down with the rest of his coffee. He looked at the other piled papers spread over his desk, rubbed a hand across his forehead, and once again

11

damned that golf club dinner.

Treasure Trove ... it came well down the list of responsibilities in the web of the Queen's and Lord Treasurer's Remembrancer's function. The antiquated title covered an organisation which, throughout all its long history, had always possessed power in a way few people dreamed existed.

Even at the beginning, when the first, medieval Remembrancer had been a bodyservant of the early Scottish kings and queens — going around with them everywhere, charged with quite literally remembering things for them.

Or occasionally forgetting, if that was more important.

A blend of walking notebook and royal conscience in the beginning, the office of Remembrancer had gradually altered in emphasis and grown.

The 1970s brand of Remembrancer was a senior grade professional civil servant who became involved in most things that mattered in Scotland. From being paymaster for every government department north of the border to constituting his own court of law in many a revenue case. From being responsible for the processing of what was vaguely termed 'state intelligence' to looking after the security of the Scottish crown jewels.

Regulation of company registrations, auditing the Scottish law courts, making sure fines in those courts were collected and paid over to the crown . . .

The list went on and on, even to making sure tax inspectors paid the right amount of income tax on their salaries.

A sudden thought came to Falconer and he glanced at his desk calendar. The fifteenth of the month — he brightened.

It was his day to sign cheques. Maybe twenty million pounds' worth, being paid out for everything from new motorways to the bill for the little man who went up and cleaned the Crown Jewels at Edinburgh Castle.

Twenty million in a day wasn't bad going for anyone.

Even with a hangover.

★ ★ ★

Two hours' flying time from London aboard a *Transportes Aeros Portugueses* jet gave Jonathan Gaunt ample opportunity to study the Department file on Francis Preston. The Boeing left London shortly after noon and by the time the 'Fasten Seatbelts' sign winked on and they began descending through heavy cloud he reckoned he'd memorised most of the essentials.

Stubbing his cigarette and stowing the file in his briefcase, Gaunt sat back and considered what mattered. At forty, Preston had been an engineer who sold out a patent on a minor steel-making process for enough money to mean he didn't have to worry too much about working. A bachelor, he'd changed what had been a hobby into a fulltime interest in archaeology.

The file listed some of the ventures that had resulted in a handful of years. They ranged from locating a Greek temple site in Cyprus and a Bronze Age fort in Germany to a nibbling attempt at salvaging a sunken Spanish *guarda costa* frigate in the Caribbean.

Nibbling was a good word, decided Gaunt. He looked out of his window as the Boeing broke cloud for a moment, showing the broad, muddy estuary of the Tagus River far below and busy with shipping. The slim thread of a four-lane suspension bridge across its neck, more than a mile in length, was new since the only other time he'd been in Portugal.

He winced at the reminder. It had been a honeymoon trip.

"Quite a sight, eh?" nudged the large, hearty Englishman who occupied the next seat and who had been trying to make conversation ever since London. He leaned across to get a better view, "That's the Salazar bridge. Any notion what that cost them?"

Gaunt shook his head, knowing it was coming anyway.

"Thirty million pounds, seventy-five million if you think in dollars." The man, who had the smooth-shaved look of a sales rep. hunting some business deal, gave a grunt of satisfied amusement. "These people may have the lowest per capita income in Europe, but they are spending money, wherever it comes from."

The jet's hydraulics began a new

gobbling noise for flaps and under-carriage while another cloud wiped out the bridge and the sprawling city below. Shrugging, the man settled back in his seat, while Gaunt wondered how you rated assets like pride and tradition.

He switched his thoughts back to Francis Preston.

Nibbling . . . Preston hadn't specialised and hadn't gone in for the really big-time expeditions. He either operated alone or gathered a few people for a particular purpose, and on that basis his success to failure ratio had been surprisingly good. Good enough to lend a lot of credence to the claims he'd made for his Scottish find.

But the file told little about the rest of the man. His nearest known relative was a sister somewhere, he had no close friends, no particular attachments.

Francis Preston emerged as a solitary, perhaps even lonely man whose life had held only one passion. A passion that had killed him near a little village named Claras where the file said he'd been exploring round the site of an old Moorish fortress called Castelo de Rosa.

16

For a man like Preston, that might have been as good a way to go as any.

★ ★ ★

It was raining when the TAP Boeing landed at Lisbon International Airport, its passengers emerging from customs and immigration into a main concourse which was a damp noisy chaos. A couple of charter holiday flights, delayed on the ground, were the main trouble and the way out was through an obstacle course of scattered luggage, arguing passengers and harassed officials.

It had been that way the last time too, remembered Gaunt as he elbowed his way through to the main exit and found the airport cab rank. The lead cab was a green and black Mercedes of uncertain vintage, the driver a moon-faced character in a leather jerkin who shoved away a girlie magazine before he leaned across to open the passenger door.

"*Por favor* . . . I have to get to a village called Claras," said Gaunt, heaving his suitcase aboard and getting into the back seat. "You know it?"

"*Sim, senhor.*" Sharp eyes quickly assessed Gaunt's luggage and briefcase and were satisfied. "It is a long way, of course. Also, there is a toll on the auto-estrada . . . "

"Just get me there," said Gaunt, cutting the recital short. "I'll pay."

"Okay." The driver nodded cheerfully and started the cab. "You go to a funeral maybe, senhor?"

"That's right." Gaunt raised a surprised eyebrow, the black tie still in his briefcase. "Does it show?"

"My brother also drives an airport cab. Today he took two people from here to Claras — for a funeral, they said." Sending the Mercedes weaving out into the traffic, its tyres hissing on the wet roadway, the man bounced a grin back through the rear view mirror. "Not many people go to Claras this time of year."

"What else did your brother tell you?" asked Gaunt suddenly interested.

"They were a man and woman, both young and English." The driver took a moment to horn-blast past a lumbering truck then glanced back again. "It is a

18

long way for people to come to say *adeus*. Someone important must have died, eh?"

"Some people must think so," answered Gaunt vaguely, lighting a cigarette. He settled back, relieved to know he was guaranteed some company at Preston's graveside. "What size of a place is Claras?"

"Small, senhor . . . very small. Tourists in the summer maybe, but in the winter there is nothing." His driver took one hand from the wheel and waved expansively, ignoring the bustling traffic. The cab had a posy of plastic flowers in a tiny holder and a small crucifix had been glued above the ignition switch. "They say there are big plans for Claras, but in Portugal we always have plans — more plans than money."

Gaunt nodded and fell silent, stifling a grimace as a familiar dull ache stabbed again in his back, the way it had been doing on and off for the past half hour.

Travel ache, the specialists called it. One of the things to expect after a broken back.

Two years had passed since a partial

19

'chute failure in a training jump had nearly killed Lieutenant J. Gaunt of the Parachute Regiment. After six months recovering in a military hospital he'd been discharged — to a disability pension and a wife who wanted a divorce.

Patti, who was someone else's wife now — though he couldn't get used to that part.

The cab took a roundabout without slowing, the traffic thicker than ever. On a little platform in the middle of the roundabout, a points policeman wore a plastic raincoat with his white sun helmet.

Gaunt smiled absently, realising the rain was still drizzling down. He still couldn't blame Patti. She'd been young, she'd married a pair of paratroop wings, she hadn't hinted things were wrong till after he was out of hospital.

They'd even managed to finish almost amicably, with no family to add extra strain . . .

He pushed that part out of his mind, the ache stabbing again. The last medical board had cut his army pension, reckoning his back was improving. The painkiller pills he had to carry were incidental, as incidental as the occasional nightmares that still came. Nightmares when he was falling again, always waking just before he hit the ground.

The worst time for them had been after the divorce. He'd been drifting, his only nebulous asset a few University terms spent studying law and accountancy before he'd gone into the army.

Then somebody, somewhere, had a contact, the Queen's and Lord Treasurer's Remembrancer had called him for an interview . . . and he'd gone on the payroll.

Things could have worked out worse. Jonathan Gaunt, thirty-four years of age, unattached, and living again, was enjoying most of it. Gathering some fresh interests, like the potent little Mini-Cooper he ran on a shoe-string. Or playing the stock market for a new brand of small-time excitement, usually on an overdraft.

Like now — the last thing he'd done before he left home. There was a hint of a reverse takeover involving a couple of English breweries. He'd sold a bundle of low-cost African tin shares, caught in the aftermath of a presidential coup, switching the money to take an option on a thousand brewery shares.

By the time he returned they'd either be ripe for a profit or he'd have to live on beans for a couple of months.

But what the hell? He was living, and that was what mattered.

* * *

Skirting Lisbon, the route to Claras started as a long concrete slash of busy auto-estrada with heavy traffic pouring in both directions. That ended near Estoril, where the rain had stopped and the sun was steaming the roads dry. The cab purred through the resort's clustered hotels, the highway running along the edge of the shore where sandy beaches were backed by unbroken blue Atlantic.

Then they swung inland again, small villages and fields punctuated by white, wide-sailed windmills rapidly giving way to rising, wooded country. At last, leaving the main highway at a sign for Claras, the cab followed a narrow, winding road down towards a little township of red roofs and white walls. It had a tall church spire near the middle and several large villas were scattered around its tree-fringed outskirts.

Gaunt glanced at his watch. Little more than an hour had passed since they'd left Lisbon, which was better than he'd hoped. Leaning forward, he tapped the moon-faced driver's shoulder.

"Find the cemetery first, then an hotel."

"*Sim, senhor.*" The man grinned and nodded. "No problem. There is only one of each in this place."

For Claras's size that seemed enough. The cemetery was on the way in, a small neat patch of ground with two broad-leafed palm trees at its entrance. From there a couple of minutes brought them to the village square and the cab pulled in at the Hotel Da Gama, a three-storey building with balconied windows and an ornately tiled doorway.

Gaunt got out, collected his suitcase, and stonily paid a fare which was probably twice what he should have been charged. Then, as the green and black Mercedes accelerated away in a scatter of dust, he looked round.

Claras seemed deserted. A few cars, an old truck and a couple of donkey carts were parked beside a small fountain in the middle of the cobbled square. But the only people were two women in black gossiping outside a bakery shop and a man in a sports shirt and sunglasses lounging at a pavement café table.

Picking up the suitcase, Gaunt went into the Da Gama's cool, dark lobby. He had to ring a bell before the reception clerk, who was thin and balding, emerged from somewhere at the rear still pulling on his jacket.

"Senhor?" The man had bad teeth but the smile was friendly enough.

"I need a room, probably for a couple of nights," Gaunt told him.

"*Por favor . . .* " the desk clerk frowned, looked around and shouted. "Jaime!"

The boy who answered was still in his early teens. Brown skinned, lanky, and with a mop of jet black hair, he wore slacks, a torn white sweatshirt and leather sandals. After listening to the desk clerk's

24

mutter he grinned, turning to Gaunt.

"You wish a room, senhor? I speak English."

"Yes, for tonight or maybe longer," nodded Gaunt.

The hotel register was pushed towards him. He took his time signing, noting the two names immediately above his own. A Mr and Mrs John Marsh had booked in, taking a double room with bath and giving the curt address, "Liverpool, England."

When he turned, the boy had his suitcase and a room key. Gaunt followed him, the youngster whistling cheerfully as he led the way up a carpeted stairway to the top floor. The room was near the end of the corridor, the window shutters closed. But as they were swung open sunlight flooded in on a bed that looked clean and comfortable and furnishings which were plain but sturdy.

"You look out on the square," volunteered the boy. "Okay?"

"Fine," agreed Gaunt. "You're Jaime?"

"Yes, senhor." The boy opened the last shutter and faced him, smiling.

"Maybe you can help me then, Jaime.

I've come to Claras for a funeral — the funeral of an Englishman named Preston. Did you know him?"

The smile vanished and Jaime nodded.

"He was a good man," he answered seriously. "I liked him — he and his friends came here often in the evening." A grimace crossed his face. "Senhor Preston would laugh and joke, but his friends were not always so happy — or so liked."

"I never met him," admitted Gaunt. "But I'll take your word for it. How many other guests in the hotel are here for the funeral?"

"None, senhor." The youngster shrugged a little. "Two did arrive this morning, but then Doctor Sollas came to see them and they went off with him instead."

"Who's this man, Sollas?"

"A *medico* . . . a doctor. He came with Senhor Preston to be his partner in the digging at the Castelo," explained Jaime patiently. "The digging people rent a villa outside Claras — I think maybe he took those two to stay with him there."

"I'll need to meet Doctor Sollas," mused Gaunt. "What does he look like?"

"A big man, big like a bull," said the youngster almost grimly. "He has a scar, like this" — he traced a finger across the bridge of his nose — "and a loud voice. He is easy to recognise."

"Good." Going over to the window, Gaunt went out on the little balcony beyond the glass and looked down at the cobbled square. There were now three women gossiping outside the shop, but the man in sunglasses had vanished.

"Jaime, how far away is this Castelo de Rosa?"

"A few kilometres — you can almost see it from here. There is a hill to your left, okay? The Castelo is there, an old watchtower place halfway up, among the trees." The boy hesitated. "You know the funeral is at four o'clock, senhor?"

"Yes." Gaunt nodded, his eyes on the wooded, hog-backed hill and the higher peaks which lay beyond it. "Thanks."

"Obrigado, senhor." The boy went out quietly, clicking the room door shut.

Gaunt stayed on the balcony. The man in sunglasses had appeared again, coming from immediately below him as if leaving the hotel. Walking briskly, the figure headed across the square then his bright sports shirt vanished up a side-street.

Shrugging, Gaunt returned to the room, opened his suitcase, and unpacked a little. Then, the ache in his back still a low-key throb, he sprawled out on the bed and smoked a cigarette.

At last, as the hands of his watch came round towards four, he got up again. A wash left him feeling fresher as he put on the black tie and checked its knot in the mirror. Grimacing at his reflection, he checked that his cigarettes were back in his pocket and set off.

Downstairs, the hotel lobby was deserted. But a few more people were moving around in the square as he went out and started in the direction of the cemetery.

It was a pleasant walk. Claras liked colour. It was there in the brightly painted woodwork of its little houses with their clean stucco walls and ornate roofs, in the gay flower boxes outside every window, but above all in the glazed *azulejo* picture tiles which framed most doorways.

Some were built in elaborate mural panels, often with a religious theme, others formed pure geometric patterns of clean, cool blue and white. That other time he'd been in Portugal he and Patti had seen *azulejo* tiles in plenty. But never so many, never so varied. In Claras, they were an art form.

Strolling on, the sun warm between his shoulders, Gaunt had the cemetery in sight ahead when the sound of cars approaching made him look round. A small convoy of vehicles was coming towards him.

In another moment the lead vehicle went past. An elderly motor hearse with black paintwork and tarnished chrome, it carried a polished oak coffin topped by several wreaths.

Behind it came two large limousines filled by an assortment of dark-garbed mourners then, like a rearguard, four men in a battered green jeep. They were a quartet with solemn, sun-tanned peasant faces and wore clean work clothes with black arm-bands.

The funeral cortege reached the entrance gates and turned in. Quickening his pace, Gaunt was almost there too when another car swept up, travelling fast in a way which made him sidestep quickly towards the hedge of prickly pear which lined the opposite side of the road.

He had a brief glimpse of a small red Lancia coupé with a woman behind the wheel. She was young and good-looking, with long, raven-black hair caught back by a silver clasp, but before more could register the car had gone, a brisk gearchange being followed by a spurt of gravel and dust from its tyres as it followed the others into the cemetery driveway.

Plodding on, Gaunt entered the gates. Ahead, the red Lancia had pulled up behind the other vehicles at the far side of the cemetery where a clump of almond trees were in dazzling white blossom. Already grouped beside a new mound of chalk-streaked earth, the mourners were waiting while the coffin, brass handles glinting in the sunlight, was carried over from the hearse.

Reaching the Lancia, which had a tiger-cat transfer snarling from its trunk lid, Gaunt stopped and watched as the service got under way.

It was in English, with a priest

officiating who wore Church of England robes. But the words reached him as little more than a murmur and he ignored them, considering the mourners instead. The girl from the Lancia, a black lace shawl now over her hair, stood a little apart from the others. Slim and tall, wearing a coffee coloured dress, she glanced round twice towards the car and each time gave a slightly puzzled frown in his direction before she turned away.

A second girl, fair-haired and younger, was among the small group closest to the graveside. In a cream suit with a black, wide-brimmed hat, she gave an impression of only detached interest in the whole proceedings but looked away for a moment as the coffin was lowered.

The clergyman's voice sounded again, his hand rose in a symbolic sprinkling of earth, then the mourners fell back and the gravediggers picked up their shovels.

The thud of soil on hollow wood was already under way as the little group began to drift back towards the cars. Two of the men stopped to speak to the girl from the Lancia but though she smiled at them, she shook her head at what they said.

One figure was moving more purposefully. A big man in a dark suit, with thinning, mousey hair, he strode towards Gaunt with an expression of wary curiosity on his heavy features.

And he had a scar across his nose. Gaunt went to meet him.

"Doctor Sollas?" he asked.

"That's right." The voice was a booming rumble and Sollas's blue eyes were cool in their appraisal. "I saw you standing back here. Were you a friend of Preston's?"

"No." Gaunt shook his head.

"Then . . . ?" Arthur Sollas's manner chilled several degrees.

"I was sent." Gaunt shrugged apologetically and brought out his Remembrancer's Office identification card. "The timing wasn't my idea — but it may save complications."

"I see." The big man's scowl made it plain he didn't as he examined the card. "All right, Mr Gaunt, what's it all about? If you're some kind of tax vulture . . . "

"No." Gaunt stopped him with a quick, fractional smile. "You could say it's more the other way round. My job is to talk to Preston's colleagues and friends — and any relatives I can find. Somebody could be feeling very happy by the time I'm finished."

The scowl faded but Arthur Sollas still treated him with a chilly caution.

"I'd like to know why," he said bluntly, with a glance back over his shoulders. "Most people would at least wait till a man's grave was filled in."

"I'm not exactly stopping that," said Gaunt patiently. "But I want to make sure people know I'm here — let them know before they scatter again." He shrugged mildly. "No harm in that, is there?"

"Depends what you want, doesn't it?" countered Sollas grimly.

"Information," Gaunt told him. "If we get the kind we want then it could mean someone collecting a sizeable amount of money."

"From the British Government?" Arthur Sollas gave a humourless grin of disbelief.

"Taxpayers' money," nodded Gaunt.

"We draw the line at using our own." He paused, meeting Sollas's gaze cheerfully. "Would it help if I said we were specifically interested in Treasure Trove — and what Francis Preston was doing in Scotland last year?"

"It — yes, it might." Arthur Sollas rubbed a slow, thoughtful finger along his scarred nose, his manner thawing. Then he gave a grunt of near amusement. "Yes, I'd say it makes things a lot clearer. Give me a moment." He turned and raised his voice. "Carlos . . . "

A thin, pock-faced individual, one of the workmen who'd arrived aboard the jeep, trotted over.

"Take the men back to camp. *Immediatamente* . . . I don't want them diving into a bar somewhere. And Carlos, I'll want to see you later." As the man nodded his understanding and turned away, Sollas switched his attention back to Gaunt. "They're from our digging team — though right now I've stopped all work. In fact, we've still to decide whether we go on or just pack it all in. You know Preston was killed at the site?"

Gaunt nodded. "That's all we heard.

What happened?"

Sollas shook his head bleakly. "The one damned fool thing Preston kept warning everybody else not to do. He went wandering around the site on his own late at night, after dark. Either he fell into part of the main trench or it caved in while he was down in it — but we found him in the morning, under about ten feet of muck."

Behind them, the Lancia's engine suddenly rasped to life. Gaunt swung at the sound and saw the raven-haired girl was back behind the wheel. Dark, strangely questioning eyes in a face which was beautiful yet somehow strained met his own for an instant. Then her lips tightened and the car began moving.

"Well, I've things to do right now." Sollas spoke again as the Lancia drew away. "Where are you staying, Gaunt?"

"In Claras — I've a room at the Hotel Da Gama."

"That's handy enough." Sollas gave a casual flick at a fly which came buzzing near his face. "Suppose you come out to our place tonight, about nine — the villa, not the camp? Anyone will show you where it is, and we can talk then."

The jeep, its crew aboard, was also growling off and the Lancia had just disappeared through the cemetery gates. Pointedly, Gaunt considered the handful of mourners who remained. "Will everybody be there?"

"Everybody you're likely to want to meet," said Sollas shortly.

"Doctor" — Gaunt took the chance while he had it — "how much do you know about that Scottish trip?"

"That can wait." The man grinned a little and shook his head. "As for tonight, I'll be there with the two men who were helping us organise this dig, plus a couple of relatives who flew in for today." He gestured caustically towards a young man with long, mousey hair and a dark suit who was standing beside the blonde girl. "That's Preston's nephew, John Marsh — the girl is his wife. Five minutes with them and you find it easy enough to guess what brought them galloping over. But — anyway, is that enough for you?"

"It makes a start," declared Gaunt hopefully.

"Good." Arthur Sollas drew a deep breath, as if relieved that part was over. "The villa tonight, then — right now I've got to get that damned clergyman started for home. We had to fetch him out from one of the English churches in Lisbon and he's itching to get back."

Turning on one heel, the bulky figure strode away.

Left on his own, Gaunt lit a cigarette and stayed where he was for a moment. Then, feeling he'd made a reasonable start, he set off along the gravelled driveway towards the road.

He had reached the gates when the two limousines and their returning mourners overtook him again. As the first car purred out, turning onto the roadway, Arthur Sollas raised a hand in greeting from the front passenger seat.

The second limousine followed. But as they began to pull away two figures sprang into sight behind the hedge of prickly pear on the opposite side of the road.

A shout rang out, two large stones flew through the air — and there was a crash of glass as one of the stones shattered the first limousine's windscreen.

It skidded to a halt. There was another bang as the second limousine, brakes squealing, slammed into its rear — while the two stone-throwers, youngsters in their teens, were already running from the hedge to the start of a patch of thick woodland.

Gaunt began running too. He reached the scene as Doctor Sollas tumbled out of the first limousine with livid fury on his face and a small cut trickling blood down one cheek.

"Damn them!" Sollas shook an impotent fist in the direction of the two figures, already vanishing among the trees. Then, as more of the shaken passengers appeared he grimly dismissed the matter. "Let them go. We wouldn't have a chance of catching them in there."

"You mean we just let them get away with it?" protested a voice indignantly. A bald man with peeling sunburn pushed forward. "Look, Doc, suppose we try . . . "

"I said forget it," snarled Sollas. "Is anyone hurt?"

The group looked at each other then

shook their heads. Sollas turned, took another glance at the two limousines, and was satisfied.

"They can still be driven. We'll move on." He came over to Gaunt. "You saw those damned hooligans?"

Gaunt nodded. "But not well enough to pick them out, if that's what you mean."

"It's always that way," said Sollas bleakly, dabbing at his cut with a handkerchief.

"Meaning this has happened before?" asked Gaunt with some surprise.

"Other things have." Sollas pursed his lips. "Not everyone around here likes us."

"Why?"

"Ask them," grated Sollas. He looked at the blood on his handkerchief and cursed. "Some of them just don't like strangers. Others go around with a crazy story that we're waking ghosts — but I'll tell you this. The first of those characters we catch will wish he'd never been born."

"But they've been trying to frighten you off."

Sollas bristled. "Nobody scares me off, Gaunt. I leave when I'm ready, not before."

The last of his companions had gone back aboard the limousines. Sollas strode over and climbed into his seat beside the driver of the lead vehicle, who still looked shaken. More glass showered out as he cleared loose fragments from the windscreen, then the engine fired and it grated into gear.

It moved away, the second limousine following and neither driver wasting time.

Left alone again, Gaunt looked at the glass scattered across the roadway and shrugged.

He'd meant it when he told Sollas he couldn't have identified the stone-throwers again. But one had been lanky, with a mop of black hair and a white sweatshirt. It might have been Jaime, the young porter from the Da Gama — or someone near enough his double.

But possibility held its own dangers in Sollas's present mood, quite apart from his own instinctive curiosity to find out more about the reason behind what had happened.

A fat, black-backed scavenging beetle suddenly appeared beside his feet, weaving an excited path through the glinting fragments in search of food. Mandibles quivering, it stopped where a tiny splash of blood from Sollas's cut cheek had landed on the tarmac.

Gaunt raised his foot in disgust, ready to crush it. Then he stopped and turned away with a grimace, remembering his own reason for being involved.

Though that could wait till evening now. For the moment he was more conscious of the afternoon's heat, the way his sweat-soaked shirt was sticking to his back and the dry, dusty taste gathering in his throat.

Taking a last glance towards the trees he started back down the sun-baked road towards the village.

2

CHILDREN were playing barefoot round the edge of Claras's fountain when Jonathan Gaunt got back to the cobbled square. He watched their laughing antics for a moment, envying the way they splashed in and out of the bubbling water, then made his way thankfully into the cool shadow of the Hotel Da Gama's lobby.

As usual, it was empty. But the bar was on the left and he pushed his way through a beaded curtain into a long, narrow room with a few old tables and chairs and a counter which was faced in faded red leather with a black marble top.

"*Boa tarde*, Senhor Gaunt." Dark hair slicked back, a clean white jacket buttoned up to his young neck, Jaime grinned from the other side of the counter. "It is a hot day outside, eh?"

"If you've been walking — or running."

Gaunt met the grin neutrally. "What did you do, Jaime?"

"Me?" The teenager stayed unconcerned. "There was work to do in the cellar, senhor."

"Anybody helping you?" asked Gaunt.

"In the cellar?" Jaime's dark eyes showed an almost childish innocence, and he shook his head sadly. "No, I was alone. But at least it is cool down there."

"It pays to stay cool," agreed Gaunt grimly. "I'll have a beer."

"A beer — and another brandy," said a lazy, new voice behind him. "You will join me, Senhor Gaunt?"

He turned. It was the man with sunglasses and sports shirt he'd noticed earlier in the square, and the words came with a gold-toothed smile. Gaunt considered the stranger's thin, hawk-like face while the smile lingered, then nodded.

"*Obrigado.* As long as you're not selling anything."

"Me?" The man shook his head with a chuckle then snapped finger and thumb together. "Move, Jaime. A man could

43

die of thirst while you stand staring."
He turned to Gaunt again as the
youngster jerked to life. "My name is
Costa — Manuel Costa."

"Policia," muttered Jaime, busy with a
bottle.

"Sergeant of detectives in this district,"
confirmed Costa, unperturbed. He waited
until their drinks were on the counter then
spun a coin towards Jaime. "Suppose we
go over to a table, Senhor Gaunt?"

Gaunt nodded, but took a long swallow
from his beer before he followed Costa
across towards a table in a shaded corner.
Sitting down, nursing the cool, moist
glass between his hands, he raised a
quizzical eyebrow.

"Local hospitality, Sergeant?"

"In a way." Costa, a man in his
mid-thirties with a wiry build, had a
sallow complexion and long sideburns.
He sipped his drink then sucked his lips
happily. *"Ginjinha* . . . our local brandy.
Smooth yet fiery. I can recommend it."

"Right now I'll stick to beer." Grant
washed more of the thirst from his throat
and sat back with a sigh. "Well, Sergeant,
what do you want?"

44

"Just a friendly talk." Costa waved a vague hand, in no hurry. "I heard, of course, that you came to Claras for Senhor Preston's funeral. An unhappy reason." He paused, leaning forward on the table. "Yet a strange one — when you did not know him."

"Any prize for guessing who told you?" asked Gaunt. He glanced over to the bar counter, where Jaime was making a lack-lustre job of polishing glasses, and shrugged. "Do you check on every visitor, Sergeant?"

"Only the interesting ones, believe me." Costa grinned, produced a battered pack of cigarettes, and lit one using a book of matches. "I find you interesting — and unusual."

"I've been called worse." Gaunt waited calmly.

"Senhor Gaunt, I will be honest with you," said Costa patiently. "First, I find myself with a certain problem. Then you arrive — and what I hear makes me wonder if your interests might be like my own."

"You think they could be?" fenced Gaunt, wondering what was coming.

45

"Perhaps." Costa nodded hopefully. "For instance, I would say you are not a lawyer. A lawyer would not walk to a client's funeral. He would hire a car, then add the expense to his bill."

"The expense plus ten per cent," grinned Gaunt. "They're the same breed everywhere. Why didn't you do this the easy way, Sergeant — borrow a pass-key from Jaime and check my room?"

"I did." The policeman removed his sunglasses, revealing lazy brown eyes which held a faint twinkle. "You have an excellent lock on your briefcase. I would not want to damage such an item."

"Thanks," said Gaunt dryly. "All right, let's save time. Are we talking about Francis Preston?"

Costa nodded.

"Then I'll put you straight, Sergeant. I'm a plain, ordinary British civil servant sent out because Preston's death has left us with a headache. My department simply wants me to try and pick up any pieces he left behind."

"But the matter must be important?" persisted Costa.

"There's money involved — that's why

46

I'm meeting his partners tonight. But it only concerns something that happened back in Scotland."

Gaunt paused as two men in work clothes entered the bar. They ordered drinks at the counter and stayed there, gossiping with Jaime. "What's your interest, Sergeant?"

"How the man died," said Costa gloomily.

"Preston?" Gaunt fought down a whistle of surprise.

"It may be foolishness, a waste of time, I know." Costa nodded wryly. "But it is my job to be sure."

"Do they know about this at the digging camp?"

"No." Almost sheepishly, Costa shook his head. "But then, nearly all I have is what you would call a hunch."

"A hunch?" Gaunt stared at him.

"*Por favor* . . . let me explain, eh?" Costa's lazy voice took on a weary edge. "That day, Senhor Preston was at the Castelo site till afternoon. Then we know he drove into Lisbon alone and saw a few people — museum officials, a doctor, all eminently respectable. It was late evening

47

before he left to drive back to Claras."

"And then?"

"Nothing till next morning." Costa scowled at the table. "Then he was found dead at the Castelo site, buried at the bottom of a trench which had fallen in." He stopped and looked up grimly. "It could have been an accident, as people say — there had been heavy rain before and the sides might just have collapsed. Even the *medico* who did the autopsy confirmed suffocation there as the cause of death.

"But there was another injury, Senhor Gaunt. A severe bruising on the head caused by a blow . . ."

"Maybe a chunk of stone hit him during the cave-in," countered Gaunt sceptically.

"Many reasons are possible." Costa swallowed what remained of his brandy, laid down the empty glass, and considered it sadly. "But we have had trouble between the village people and Preston's men, who are outsiders — and there are stories of quarrels inside the digging camp."

"I'd heard," murmured Gaunt. "About

48

the first part, anyway."

It was Costa's turn to be surprised. Muttering under his breath, he glanced towards the bar.

"Jaime didn't tell me," said Gaunt with a mild amusement. "He's your contact, not mine."

"Jaime is anyone's contact for a few escudos," answered the sergeant with a wry disgust. "Behind that angel face lies all the natural charm of a new-born rattlesnake — a useful rattlesnake." He rubbed his chin, puzzled. "But if it wasn't Jaime . . . "

"I heard from Doctor Sollas. It was after the funeral and he'd just had a brick thrown through a limousine windscreen."

Costa winced at the news. "You saw this happen?"

"Uh-huh. There were two of them, young, and they got away." Gaunt left it at that. "He also told me about some crazy notion that the digging at the Castelo is annoying the local ghosts."

"Lights and noises — children's tales." Costa sighed and shook his head. "There are stories, and as always there are fools who will believe them. But the rest is real enough. All the ground around the Moorish fort has been fenced off, local people are turned away — and some who protested too much have been roughly handled."

"Have you done anything about it?"

"The project has full Government backing with some powerful people interested," said Costa, shrugging. "There are times when a humble sergeant of detectives must use discretion."

Gaunt chuckled his sympathy. "So this hunch you've got about Preston's death won't be particularly popular?"

"Shall we say that my superiors are dismayed?" countered Costa with a bitter cynicism. "I have been reminded that, among other things, there is the tourist trade to consider. All the guidebooks emphasise that foreigners can come to no harm in Portugal."

"I'll remember that. But I still can't help." Gaunt pushed back his chair, ready to leave. "Sergeant, do you know a dark-haired girl, good-looking — a girl who drives a red Lancia? She was at the funeral."

"Maria-Inez," answered Costa without

hesitation and brightening. "She is a *fadista*, a folk singer. Our local celebrity."

"Was she a friend of Preston's?"

Costa gave him an old-fashioned look. "Not that way, whatever you may hear. But they knew each other." He paused and his voice warmed. "Maria-Inez has a voice of gold. At the Casino in Estoril they say even the roulette wheel stops when her act begins — and, of course, she makes more money in a week than . . . than . . . "

"Than a humble sergeant of detectives collects in a year?" Gaunt rose and grinned down at him. "Where's the best place to hire a car around here?"

"Self-drive?" Costa frowned and shook his head sadly. "That could be difficult. Except" — an idea seemed to strike him — "yes, there might be a way. When would you need it?"

"From tonight, maybe for a few days."

Sucking his teeth, Costa nodded. "Then maybe I can fix something. When you are ready, look over at the police station. Okay?"

Gaunt thanked him and left. But on the way out of the bar he stopped by

51

the counter, beckoning Jaime.

"Senhor?" The youngster approached with a touch of caution.

"Just a warning," said Gaunt softly. "Never try throwing a rock at me, Jaime. Because I'll heave it straight back at you . . . and I don't miss."

Leaving the youngster open-mouthed, he walked out.

★ ★ ★

The restaurant at the Hotel Da Gama had faded velvet curtains, dark oak woodwork, and an evening menu which concentrated on seafood soaked in olive oil. Gaunt ate alone at a small table and took his time, the only other custom being a couple of salesmen more interested in wine than food and a family group celebrating a birthday.

He finished with the *Ginjinha* brandy Costa had suggested. But one fiery glass was enough as an introduction. His palate still feeling blistered, Gaunt went back up to his room and smoked a cigarette while he once again read through the Preston file.

When he reached the last page he had to admit that what he'd hoped for just wasn't there. Everything pointed to Francis Preston having been a man who combined a belief in the direct approach with little patience for diplomacy. Yet there was no hint of major trouble on any of his previous recorded projects, no suggestion that antagonism had ever stoked up against him to any kind of flashpoint — and even antagonism fell a long way short of murder.

Which left only Costa's uneasy hunch and that bruise the Portuguese sergeant declared had been found on Preston's head. Grimacing, Gaunt put the file back in his briefcase and locked it, ready to take along to the meeting at the villa. A briefcase usually made a good calling-card, a vague hint at authority — the kind he had a feeling he might need.

He left the hotel at eight-thirty. Outside, dusk had already transformed the cobbled square to a bustling life. Brightly lit open-air cafés fringed its outline, cars and trucks were parked in rows around the fountain, now a flood-lit glow, and most of Claras's inhabitants seemed to have decided that the cool, dry evening was ideal for a stroll and gossip.

Heading across the square, dodging traffic still coming in, Gaunt made his way through the strolling groups and located the police station tucked neatly round the corner of a side-street. A shoe-box architectured concrete building with iron bars on the windows and a *Policia* sign nailed above the door, it looked strong enough to withstand a siege. But what really drew his attention was the sight of a red Lancia coupé parked empty at the kerb beside the door.

The black tiger-cat sticker on the car's trunk brought a grin to his lips as he shoved open the police station door and went in. But the only figure in the front office was a sleepy-looking policeman dozing in a chair beside a wood stove. The man came awake and murmured a greeting.

"Sergeant Costa, *por favor?*" smiled Gaunt.

Nodding, the man rose and wandered

over to another door at the rear. Knocking, he opened it and went in, leaving the door open. Gaunt heard a woman's voice for a moment, another which sounded like Manuel Costa's answer her, then the conversation ended as the other officer murmured an explanation.

Manuel Costa emerged within seconds. He was escorting the girl from the Lancia and beamed a greeting.

"I came over about the car," said Gaunt, then switched his attention to the girl, suddenly in no hurry.

She looked more at ease than the last time he'd seen her. Maybe the different outfit helped — she'd changed into white trousers and a red shirt-blouse which emphasised a slim, firm-breasted figure. Her feet were in white sandals and her long black hair, gleaming under the lights, was caught back by a simple, white ribbon. A heavy gold charm bracelet was her only jewellery.

But it was her face which mattered most. Fine boned, lightly tanned, lips already framing a calm amusement at his inspection, it held a compelling beauty.

Yet there was something else, something still trapped in those clear hazel eyes . . . something he couldn't quite name.

"The car, Senhor Gaunt?" Manuel Costa took a moment to descend to such practicalities. "Yes, it is arranged."

"Good." Gaunt kept his eyes on the girl and smiled at her. "Well, at least I get a chance to say hello this time."

She nodded. "I saw you at the funeral — Manuel has told me who you are, Mr Gaunt. I am Inez Torres."

"He said Maria-Inez when I asked him," mused Gaunt.

Inez Torres laughed, a light, husky sound. "Most *fado* singers add Maria to their names — it is an old custom."

"But she was just Inez when we were children together," added Costa proudly. "Her brother and I . . . " he stopped awkwardly then switched quickly to a mock formality, "My apologies. *Menina*, Maria-Inez, may I present Senhor Jonathan Gaunt, of the English government."

"One of the hired hands," qualified Gaunt sadly. "And I'm from Scotland. There's a difference."

"I'd heard." The smile widened. "You wear kilts and blow bagpipes."

"And drink too much whisky," he completed with a grin.

"Like the Irish? I had an Irish grandfather — a sailor who ran away from his ship." Inez Torres turned away almost reluctantly to face Costa. "Manuel, I'm sorry. But I must get back — I promised."

"Then remember what I said." Costa frowned a little. "There is no reason to worry — if there was, I would know."

She kissed him lightly and unexpectedly on the cheek then held out her hand to Gaunt, the grip light and friendly. "*Adeus*, Senhor Gaunt. Maybe I will see you again."

She left them quickly. As the main door closed behind her, Costa muttered to himself then glanced at Gaunt.

"If I had known she would grow up to be like that . . . "

"Never ignore the girl next door — old Chinese proverb." Gaunt made a sympathetic noise then checked his watch. "Where do I collect this car?"

"Right here." Costa thumbed towards

the rear of the police station. "One hundred escudos a day and you pay for the gasolene. It belongs to my brother-in-law."

They went through the building and out into the yard at the rear. A small, battered Fiat, the paintwork green but rust-flaked, was parked beside a couple of patrol wagons. Climbing aboard, Gaunt tried the engine. It fired first time and sounded reasonably healthy.

"Fine." He eased back on the accelerator. "Tell your brother-in-law that he's got a deal. Now how do I get to Sollas's villa?"

"It's four, maybe five kilometres, no more." Costa gave the directions in painstaking style, then his thin face showed an unusual touch of worry. "When you are there, you will say nothing of what we talked about?"

Gaunt shook his head. "That's not my business, Sergeant."

"Good." Costa relaxed. "Though at the same time . . . "

"You want it both ways," paraphrased Gaunt, sighing. "*Adeus*, Sergeant. I said it wasn't my business."

He flicked the Fiat into gear and set it moving, out of the yard towards the street. Behind him, Costa gave a satisfied grin, lit a cigarette, then made a leisurely return to his office.

Sergeant Manuel Costa always felt happier when he knew someone else was doing his legwork.

★ ★ ★

Gaunt's destination was north-east of Claras, out along a narrow, winding strip of mainly dirt road fringed by pine trees and scrub vegetation. Dusk had blended into night quickly enough for him to need the Fiat's lights, but the moon was out and over to his left he could see he was travelling almost parallel with the black, hump-shaped hill where the Moorish fort was located.

He tried to remember his history. It was sometime about the start of the eighth century that the Moors had come storming across from North Africa into Portugal, overrunning the entire country for a spell then stubbornly fighting off generation after generation of Crusader armies bent on freeing it from Moslem rule.

Stubborn was the word. The Moors had retained a substantial foothold right up into the thirteenth century — and five hundred years was long enough for any invasion to leave a long-term imprint on a nation's character. Long enough, too, to lay down a rich fascination of artifacts for any latter-day archeologist with a digging urge.

A roe deer flickered across the road ahead, a brief vision in the Fiat's headlamps. Portugal was supposed to have wolves up in its north, he remembered. But this was gentler country.

Unless Costa's hunch was right and a killer on two legs was on the loose around Claras.

Gaunt grimaced at the thought, reached for a cigarette, then decided against it as lights appeared through the trees ahead. Another couple of minutes and he was turning off into a short driveway.

The house at its end was a large, white, two-storey villa with a pillared main entrance and a long balcony. Three large, smartly expensive cars were parked outside and the Fiat rolled into place beside them like a poor relation in search of a handout.

Leaving it, Gaunt walked towards the flight of steps which led to the villa's doorway. The night was warm, he could hear crickets sawing in the grass around, and music was coming from a radio in one of the rooms above. The steps creaked as he climbed them and the door had an old-fashioned brass knocker in place of a bell. Rapping on it, he waited then heard men's voices on the other side of the wood. Another moment and the door swung open.

"You're punctual," boomed Arthur Sollas, looking larger than ever in the frame of light. A white strip of adhesive dressing covered the cut on his cheek and another man was standing beside him. "Come on in, Gaunt. Oh — and meet our landlord, Georges Salvador."

"Who is just leaving." Salvador was medium height and plump, sallow faced, and had dark hair and a small moustache. He wore a blue lightweight suit with a polo-necked grey silk shirt. "Senhor Gaunt. I hope you enjoy your stay — despite the circumstances."

"Before you go, Georges, have we left any loose ends?" demanded Sollas. He added for Gaunt's benefit, "Georges has been transferring the lease over from Preston's name to mine — I like to be sure of things."

"Everything we need is done," assured Salvador then, glancing at his watch, made an apologetic murmur. "I should have left earlier. I have friends waiting in Estoril — visitors with money burning a hole in their pockets and the Casino tables waiting to solve the problem."

"They'll be lucky to get out with their shirts," grunted Sollas.

"Probably." Salvador chuckled at the thought. "Doctor, I'll bring any papers that need to be signed later. But the matter is agreed. Good night."

He left them, went down the steps and over to a blue Jaguar saloon, and waved before he climbed aboard. The cars lights blinked on, then as its engine fired and it purred away, Sollas gave a grunt of relief.

"One problem less. He could have tossed us out on our ears — Preston

62

signed the lease agreement on his own, which might have been awkward."

"He chose a nice place." Gaunt looked appreciatively along an oak-panelled hallway with a polished parquet floor and animal-skin rugs. An open-plan stairway curved from half-way along towards the upper floor. "Does Salvador usually live here?"

"No, but he will once we leave." As the Jaguar's tail lights disappeared from the driveway Sollas closed the house door. "The last owners left a few months back, but Salvador doesn't want to move in till summer. That's how we got the villa." The big man came closer and lowered his voice to a confidential rumble. "I've told the others who you are, Gaunt — but not much more. They're all in the main lounge."

"Fine." Gaunt nodded cheerfully and hefted his briefcase. "Let's hope I strike lucky."

"They probably feel the same," grunted Sollas. A look of puzzled distaste crossed his broad face. "I still think this could have waited, but now you're here, let's get it over."

Leading the way down the hall, he opened a glass-panelled door and waved Gaunt through. On the other side was a large room with a high, frescoed ceiling and broad windows which were flanked by floor-length curtains of dark red velvet.

The five people already in the room stopped anything they were doing as he entered and swung their attention his way. One was the blonde girl he'd seen at the cemetery, the four men with her had all been with the funeral party, and all except the bald man with sunburn, who was over at a cocktail cabinet, were seated in leather armchairs which had been arranged with precision in a semi-circle facing a small table with a waiting, empty chair behind it.

The mood in the room was relaxed and underlined by the group's casual clothes and the drinks in their hands. But Gaunt still felt himself under close inspection as Arthur Sollas nudged him forward.

"Better start with introductions," said Sollas gruffly.

"We know who he is, so why not give him a drink first?" suggested a cheerfully sardonic voice from one of the chairs. The man who had spoken was young but almost white-haired, a lanky figure with reddened skin stretched tight across high cheekbones. He grinned at Gaunt. "I'd call that a reasonable priority."

"I wouldn't complain about it," confirmed Gaunt easily.

"Sorry." Sollas gave an irritated grunt. "Whisky, Gaunt? I don't guarantee the blend."

"Sounds fine," agreed Gaunt, looking around.

"I'll get it," volunteered the bald man at the cocktail cabinet. "On its own, Scottish style?"

"With water — I'm a renegade." Gaunt kept the smile on his lips.

"Introductions," said Sollas doggedly as the bald man began pouring. "Starting from your left, Bernard Ryan, our photographer and supply officer . . . "

"Known as Bernie." The white-haired younger man raised a hand in greeting. "But this happens to be my first digging caper so whatever you want, friend, pass on."

Pursing his lips, Sollas gestured again.

65

"Then our site foreman, Carlos Pereira. He's here because of another matter we've been discussing."

"Senhor Gaunt . . . " Pereira, his pock-marked face woodenly devoid of expression, nodded politely. The sleeves of his coarse plaid wool shirt were rolled up, showing hairy, muscular forearms tanned dark by the sun except for a pale strip across one wrist where he might normally wear a wristwatch. "Ah . . . maybe I should go now, Doctor?"

"Finish your drink first." Sollas drew a deep breath as the bald man took that as a cue to bring over Gaunt's glass. "Next, this is Martin Lawson — a professional in the archaeology game. In fact, the only professional among us."

"But still a paid hand like Ryan and Carlos." Lawson smiled mildly as he handed over the glass. "Preston and Doctor Sollas organised this dig — I was just happy to come along. We wouldn't be here but for them."

"I'm trying to forget that," said Sollas wearily. He paused as Gaunt sipped the whisky, then forced a brighter note. "Last, but maybe the people who'll interest you

66

most, Preston's relatives."

"His only relatives," emphasised the slender young man with the long mousey hair. Rising from his chair he held out a hand. The grip, Gaunt found, was moist with sweat while the faint smile on his face had a nervous quiver at the edges. "I'm John Marsh — Uncle Frank was my mother's brother, and my mother died a few months ago. So I'm all the family he had left. Ah — this is my wife, Sarah."

The blonde stayed where she was but murmured a greeting. Seen in close-up, she was still pretty in a china-doll way but her eyes were small and greedy and her full figure, several pounds overweight, wasn't helped by a loose sweater and tight black ski-pants.

"I didn't know your uncle," said Gaunt, facing Marsh again. "But from what I've heard he was the kind of man people will certainly miss."

"We didn't see much of him," said Marsh almost indifferently. "To be honest, we didn't even know he was out here — not till we heard he'd died on the job."

Behind them, the blonde stifled a

sudden giggle then looked away and reached for her drink.

"Doctor Sollas made a bit of a mystery about you, Gaunt," declared Marsh quickly. "But you want to do some kind of deal, right?"

"You could put it that way." Gaunt glanced at Sollas. "I can start anytime, Doctor."

"We're ready." Sollas waved towards the table in the centre. "If you've any papers to spread around . . ."

"That might come later." Gaunt went over and drew out the chair while Sollas nodded at Pereira and thumbed towards the door.

"*Obrigado*, Carlos. You know what we're doing. Tell the men they'll be at work again tomorrow and that they'll get full pay as usual for this week. That should keep them happy."

Grinning, the foreman rose and went out. Sollas slumped his heavy figure down into the vacated armchair.

"You're going to continue?" asked Gaunt.

"Yes." Sollas made it a rumble and rubbed a finger across his scarred nose.

"Why throw away nearly three months' slogging when we're nearly finished? There would be no damned sense in it."

"Not after all the trouble you and Preston went through to get those government permits," murmured Martin Lawson in dutiful support. "The Portuguese have their charm, Gaunt — but they operate like the mills of God. When it comes to action they grind exceeding slow."

"We think you're great too, Martin," drawled Bernie Ryan. "Now shut up, will you?"

Lawson flushed, the colour going up to match the red of his bald, peeling head. But he stayed silent, leaving Ryan to grin a little and light a cigarette.

"This was basically Frank Preston's project," said Sollas, frowning down at the floor and ignoring the exchange. "We'll miss him — but the work that is left shouldn't pose problems."

"Any chance of another member of the family stepping in?" Gaunt posed the question casually to John Marsh.

"Me?" The dead man's nephew gave

a yelp of protest. "No. I'm a salesman — groceries, on the wholesale side. Every minute I'm here is costing me money as it is. Right, Sarah?"

"We've done our duty coming to the funeral," declared the blonde with equal indignation. "We know John's the only heir. But a London lawyer is handling that side so why should we wait?" She stopped and switched to a forced smile. "Unless we can help you, of course, Mr Gaunt."

"Let's find out," said Gaunt dryly, his dislike for the couple growing rapidly. "Your uncle was in Scotland at the start of last year. What do you know about his trip?"

"Not much." Marsh looked puzzled. "He sent us a postcard, that's all."

"Where was he when he sent it?"

"Can't remember." Marsh exchanged an uneasy glance with his wife. "It was just one of those Highland sunset things. We — Sarah threw it in the bucket. We didn't bother to read it."

"Uncle Frank was always sending postcards," said Sarah Marsh defensively. "They didn't matter much."

"This one might have mattered a lot," said Gaunt, wooden-faced but almost liking the situation. "It could have been worth a lot of money."

The blonde went pale and stared at him. "How much?"

"Depending on what it said, up to fifty thousand pounds."

Sarah Marsh gave a low moan and seemed to shrink in her chair. Struck dumb, her husband could only stare. Even Bernie Ryan was jolted out of his cynical disinterest. The white-haired photographer laid down his cigarette and gave a soft whistle of surprise.

"The old devil — he must have meant it! Martin" — he swung towards Lawson, gesturing an appeal — "remember all that malarkey he spouted one night when we'd killed a few bottles? That crazy story about walking away from a cave-load of treasure?"

"Church plate — I remember." Licking his lips, Lawson nodded. "My God, I thought he'd just had a few too many, that it was the booze talking . . . " He stopped, awestruck.

"Doctor Sollas?" queried Gaunt quietly.

"I heard him." Arthur Sollas nodded calmly, unperturbed. "But drunk or sober, he didn't give any hint where this cave was supposed to be — only that it was in Scotland."

"That's right. And I laughed at him." Ryan shook his head despairingly. "Bernie Ryan, champion idiot — damn my luck. Martin, what about you?"

"The same." The older man shrugged with an equal gloom. "Where it was didn't matter much — I didn't believe him."

"None of us did, not for a moment." Sollas shifted his bulk in his chair to a squeak of springs. "Have your people any reason that makes them feel differently, Gaunt?"

"All I know is he convinced them." Gaunt drank more of his whisky with mixed emotions. "But if it does exist then that hoard rates as Treasure Trove. We'll pay out to the first person who can take us to it."

"The first?" Sarah Marsh seized on the point with a gasp of indignation. "But if John's uncle found this treasure then surely John . . . "

"No." Gaunt stopped her firmly. "Preston had no rights to the plate and knew it. That doesn't change — the stuff belongs to the Crown and we're simply offering a reward for help."

"Damn the Crown." She had a new idea. "Suppose John's uncle left a map somewhere, a diary — anything like that?"

"Yes." Her husband brightened at the thought. "That would be different, wouldn't it?"

"You'd have a claim on the reward — if you had legal ownership of the details."

"Right!" John Marsh's pasty face showed triumph. "Doctor — my Uncle Frank's gear is still upstairs, isn't it?"

"Packed ready to move," confirmed Sollas dryly. "But I didn't notice any map with an 'X' on it."

"Mind if we have a look?" asked Marsh eagerly.

Shrugging, Sollas reached into his pocket and brought out a key-ring. He looked at it for a moment then tossed it on the table with something close to scorn.

"Go ahead," he invited.

"Thanks." Marsh rose quickly and scooped up the keyring. Then, as his wife joined him, he hesitated, glancing at the others. "I mean — well, we want to find out, don't we?"

"Straight away." said Bernie Ryan acidly. "Don't trip on the stairs, friend."

Grinning weakly, Marsh turned to his wife and nodded. They went out quickly, the door banging shut behind them.

"Half a chance, and they'd have Preston out of that grave to go through his pockets." Ryan swore softly but pungently then sighed and rose lazily. "To hell with them. I've still got work to do."

"Those equipment lists." Sollas nodded absently. "Help him, Martin. Now we're starting again I don't want any hold-ups we can avoid."

Obediently, Lawson followed the photographer from the room. Left alone with Gaunt, Sollas grimaced his disgust.

"We all have relatives, I suppose," he said with a surprising mildness. "Still, they're wasting their time. I went through Preston's kit and didn't find anything." He saw Gaunt's raised eyebrow and twisted a smile in reply. "Just an old army habit — never leave shocks for the next-of-kin."

"You thought there might have been?" queried Gaunt.

"He had a friend in Claras — she was at the funeral."

"I noticed."

"I don't think it was that way with them, but I just made sure." Spreading his thick fingers, Sollas levered up from his chair. "Anyway, while you're here, come through to the office. I'll show you what brought him to Portugal."

He led the way out of the lounge and through to a small study near the back of the villa. It held two desks, one now conspicuously bare and the other covered in papers. Trestle tables had been set up round the walls and carried an accumulation of charts, and reference books mixed with fragments of tile and pottery.

Crossing to the paper-littered desk, Arthur Sollas opened a drawer and brought out an unframed photograph.

"That's what he was like," he said shortly.

The photograph showed a stocky, middle-aged man with a bearded, handsome face and a piratical grin. He was sitting on a rock, wearing only shorts and sandals, a can of beer in one hand.

"How well did you know him?" asked Gaunt, studying the print.

"We'd met a few times." Sollas flicked the photograph back in the drawer. "I'm another hobby archaeologist — the practice of medicine pays my bills." He shrugged. "Preston wanted someone to split the cost on this dig and contacted me through Lawson — he already had Ryan lined up."

"Preston had a fair reputation for choosing a site," mused Gaunt, looking round the rest of the room. "How has it been here?"

The big man eyed him oddly then made the nose-stroking motion which always seemed to precede a decision.

"We didn't come to play around what's left of a second-rate Moorish watchtower," he said slowly. "You'll find plenty the same all over this damned country."

"Then . . . "

"You'd have to know Preston to understand." Sollas went over to the nearest bench and unrolled one of the charts. "His genius was that he knew damn-all about conventional archaeology. Preston was an engineer and he thought like an engineer — local geography, materials, construction, all from a slightly different angle. One that usually paid off."

Gaunt frowned down at the opened chart. It showed two outlines, one small and firm, the other still with broken lines but considerably larger. Puzzled, he tried to understand.

"You're working on something better?"

Arthur Sollas nodded. "Preston saw photographs of this watch-tower and had a hunch it was different, that the Moors might have built on an earlier site, using existing material." A stubby finger traced round the larger outline. "We've uncovered a second century B.C. Roman villa nobody dreamed was there. As far as Preston was concerned even that was a disappointment — he thought we'd find something bigger." His voice hardened a shade. "But the villa is important enough, and I don't want any outside leak about it till we're ready to start shouting."

"I'd like to see the place," murmured Gaunt. His attention switched to a large-scale map pinned on the wall. "Can I come visiting — or do I have to pass a loyalty test first?"

"Make it tomorrow, after breakfast, and I'll show you around." Sollas tapped the map. "We're here right now. Branch off the route you came at about two kilometres back, stick with the side-road till you come to a fork, then veer right — you'll find it's a fairly rough track. We're where it ends, or where it ends now at any rate. I told you we had to close a route."

"Something which didn't make you popular," mused Gaunt.

"We've enough problems without the locals clumping around the diggings." Sollas scowled at the notion. "Give those people half a chance and they'd loot anything they could carry — then sell it to tourists later. We've got to be careful, Gaunt. The Portuguese government made a tough deal — Preston had to promise we'd settle for glory and knowledge, with anything recovered belonging to the State. Any trouble, and they'd be down on our necks — particularly now."

It sounded familiar enough. Gaunt gave a sympathetic grin. "So you won't be too upset about those ghost stories scaring people away?"

"We didn't start them, if that's what you're hinting. But whoever had the notion did us a favour." Sollas glanced at his watch then yawned deliberately. "Ten-thirty already — well, whatever that pair of married vultures are scavenging for upstairs, I'm for bed. I need an early night."

"I feel the same." Gaunt let Sollas steer him out of the room then, as the door closed behind them, mused almost to himself, "Still, I'm curious about the way Preston died. I thought you'd have a night watchman at the site?"

"The digging squad take the job in turn." Sollas scowled at the thought as they started down the hallway. "Usually with a bottle of wine for company — the idiot on duty that night woke up about dawn, saw Preston's car parked at the gate, and went into a squealing panic when he found the main trench caved in.

"And nobody missed Preston till then?" asked Gaunt.

"Get something straight, Gaunt . . ." The big man came to an irritated halt. "This isn't a Boy Scout camp. We don't operate any kind of lights out bed-call. We knew Preston had gone into Lisbon on personal business and what he did afterwards was his affair." His lips pursed angrily. "Usually when he didn't show up it meant he'd gone off on a drinking kick — I didn't see the autopsy report, but I'll bet it showed he'd enough alcohol in him to pickle an elephant."

"I didn't know," soothed Gaunt.

"Why should you have?" Sollas strode on till he reached the front door of the villa, swung it open, then shook his head bitterly. "It was a damned waste of a life, Gaunt. Why shout about the details and make it worse?"

Saying good night, Gaunt left. Back aboard the Fiat, he started the engine and slipped the little car into gear. As it moved off, Arthur Sollas's bulky figure was still framed in the villa doorway.

* * *

Spring in Portugal can mean crisp, chill nights with a sky like moonspun velvet then a milky fog around dawn. The velvet was overhead as Jonathan Gaunt steered the Fiat along the dirt road, the briefcase he hadn't had to open beside him in the passenger seat. His thoughts drifted mutinously round what he might do if John and Sarah Marsh came up with a claim for the Remembrancer's reward money.

The more he heard about Francis Preston the more he found himself liking this man he'd never met. A man who, drunk or sober, had been driving on the same road only a few nights before, heading towards a hunch that had somehow gone wrong.

The Fiat lurched savagely over a pothole and he had to fight the wheel to avoid landing in the ditch. Gaunt grimaced as the car steadied, deciding

Preston couldn't have been so drunk if he'd been able to handle a car in these conditions.

The dark bulk of the hogback hill began growing on the right while he mulled over the thought, warier now, keeping to a slower pace and watching curiously for the turn-off he'd seen on Sollas's map. It showed in the headlamps in a couple of minutes, a black plunge into the trees. Humming softly, no particular reason in mind, Gaunt glanced beyond it, up towards the hill.

Then he swore and braked, knocking the Fiat's gear-change into neutral. Stopped there, the engine ticking gently, he wound down the Fiat's grimy side-window and looked again. Lights were moving up among the trees, three of them, working along one small section of hillside in a wavering but methodical pattern.

A moment later the harsh crack of a shot reached his ears. The flecks of light stopped, there was another shot, then they were wavering on again.

Sighing, he flicked the car back into

gear and started it on the track towards the hill. The Moorish fort might have its ghosts, but he'd never known a spirit that used a high velocity rifle when it went haunting.

3

WITHIN a minute of leaving the main road the track through the trees took a sudden dip into a world which became pitch-black as the timber thickened and leafy branches closed overhead.

Bouncing and shuddering over a surface of broken stone and loose dirt, the Fiat struggled on while its headlamp beams sent rabbits scurrying and reflected back bright eyes glaring from the protection of the trees. The fork on the map came up and he turned right, past a warning sign-board, while the new track began to climb again.

Fighting the jarring steering-wheel, he eased round a tight bend — and next moment the Fiat gave a lurch then canted wildly towards the nearside. A thud shook its way through the metal body and the engine stalled.

Shoving open the driver's door, Jonathan Gaunt climbed out, looked, and cursed.

The nearside front wheel was buried to the axle in a ditch. For a moment he stood there, tempted to give up, hearing only the soft spitting of the cooling car exhaust and the faint rustle of wind in the trees. Then, shrugging, he switched off the Fiat's lights, took the ignition key, and started off again on foot.

Stumbling through the darkness, the track still an upward climb, he'd been walking only a couple of minutes when the ground began to dip again. At the same time the trees started to thin, giving way to scattered clumps of thick, sweet-smelling scrub bush and patches of cactus. Surprisingly, the moon was still out — and the same lazy fireflies of light, now easily identifiable as hand-torch beams, were continuing their movement ahead.

The track showed as a narrow ribbon, wandering down the gentle reverse slope towards a gate in a high fence. Two tin-roofed huts were located behind the gate and beyond them an intricate pattern of long, low mounds of earth lay round the squat, roofless silhouette of a ruined tower.

The scent of woodsmoke reached his nostrils, probably from a stove in one of the huts. But Gaunt switched his attention back to the lights. They were outside the fence, over to his left, and methodically searching their way down another slope of scrub. As he watched, there was a shout, another voice answered — and immediately all three lights veered in a new direction.

Commonsense urged him to stay clear but curiosity won out. Leaving the track, he began working along the edge of the trees, heading towards the lights but keeping on the saucer rim of the slope.

A shot slammed out, not the high velocity crack he'd heard before but the duller bark of a shotgun. He froze, while the men behind the lights exchanged shouts then formed into a new pattern.

Simultaneously the moonlight gave a fleeting glimpse of something being driven ahead of them. Man or animal, it was coming nearer, making for the shelter of the trees. Heading his way.

Easing into the cover of a bush, Gaunt waited. Twigs snapped below then, suddenly, a man staggered into the middle of a band of open ground. Thin, swaying on his feet and obviously close to collapse, the hunted figure glanced back over his shoulder then tried to stumble on. Two steps forward and he fell. When he tried to rise he could only get to his knees.

So he started to crawl.

But the little drama was only beginning. Another figure appeared in the moonlight, running from the edge of the trees to Gaunt's left and still hidden from the approaching pursuit.

It was a girl — and with that long, black hair, those white trousers showing under a dark, belted raincoat and that slim silhouette it could be only one girl.

Inez Torres reached the crawling figure, stooped, put an arm round the man's waist, and pulled him upright. Then, half-dragging and half-carrying him, she started back towards the trees.

The torch-beams were still flickering through the scrub some three hundred yards away, coming on steadily and methodically. Only luck would get Inez Torres and her companion back to the trees in time — and even then they weren't likely to get much further.

Sighing, Gaunt abandoned his cover and headed across the open ground at a fast lope. Struggling on, intent on her task, the girl didn't see him until he had almost arrived. Then she gasped and swung round, placing her body like a shield between Gaunt and her burden.

"I'll take him," said Gaunt simply. Then, seeing her startled recognition, he added a quick reassurance. "It's all right. But let's get to hell out of here."

She hesitated for a moment then nodded and released her grip. Taking over, Grant discovered the frail figure weighed little more than a child might — while a sunken, young-old face stared at him with eyes which held only confusion and fear. Shifting his grip, Gaunt lifted the stranger bodily, cradled him in his arms, and started off at the same fast lope back towards the trees with Inez Torres hurrying at his side.

At most, there was eighty yards of clearing to be crossed. That was still eighty yards of being a clear, moonlit target, eighty yards when every step might bring a shout or a shot if they were spotted.

But somehow nothing happened. They reached the trees again and Gaunt swung in behind the shelter of a tangle of tall, spikey cactus. Lowering the stranger to the ground, he crouched beside him and looked back the way they had come.

For a moment the clearing stayed empty. Crouching close to him, taking short, quick breaths, Inez Torres stared in the same direction then tensed and pointed.

The first of the torch-beams had reached the opposite edge of the clearing. A burly figure strode out then came to a puzzled halt, the light's powerful glare swinging in a purposeful arc. Gaunt pursed his lips in a silent whistle as the moonlight showed the man was carrying a shotgun at the ready, the torch taped to the underside of its barrel.

See and shoot. It wasn't particularly clever if you were stalking an armed opponent. But in this kind of hunt it could be grimly effective.

Suddenly stirring, the stranger at Gaunt's feet gave a soft moan and tried to rise. Quickly, he laid a warning hand on the man's mouth — and saw him shrink back in near terror at the touch, one arm going up instinctively to ward off a blow.

"*Nao* . . . no, Luis. It's all right." The girl bent low over him, her voice an anxious murmur. As the man relaxed again, she looked up at Gaunt. "He doesn't understand. He . . . "

"He's not the only one," Gaunt cut her short. All three men who'd been hunting the stranger were now in the clearing. The two newcomers, torches similarly mounted on their guns, stood as he had for a moment then came over to join him and talk. Grimacing his relief, Gaunt glanced down at the thin figure on the ground. "I've got an edge on them now. But they'll try up here soon enough, and if he's wounded . . . "

"He isn't." She shook her head. "Not the way you mean. It — he just isn't well."

"Is he a friend?" queried Gaunt dryly.

"My brother." She bit her lip. "He hasn't done anything wrong."

"They seem to have a different idea."

Gaunt glanced down at the men again then eased round a little to face her in the tree-filtered moonlight. "Either way, we've got to get him out of here."

She nodded. "If I could get him back to my car . . . "

"Where is it?"

"Not far." She pointed in towards the black heart of the wood. "I left it hidden near the road fork and I know the way."

Gaunt remembered his own car and thought swiftly.

"Could you get him there on your own?" he asked.

Her eyes widened in surprise but she nodded.

"Then give me a couple of minutes then start moving. If things work out, wait for me on the main road just this side of Claras. All right?"

"Yes." She was puzzled. "What are you going to do?"

"Give them something else to think about. Just stay ready — and keep him quiet." He smiled at her, then started off at a low crouch, moving parallel with the edge of the trees and heading back in the direction of the track which led to the digging site.

When Gaunt judged he was halfway he rose and looked round. The men in the clearing had come to a decision. Fanned out again, they were starting up the slope towards the trees. A couple of long strides took him into the open. Waving an arm, he hailed them loudly.

"Hey, over there! *Por favor* . . . I need some help."

The torchbeams swung in startled fashion, catching him in their combined glare as he strode nearer. Keeping a grin on his face, putting one hand up to shield his eyes from the light, Gaunt kept on. As he reached the silent, waiting trio he heard a sudden grunt of recognition from one of them.

"Senhor Gaunt . . . " the man lowered his gun and stepped forward. It was Pereira, the digging team foreman, and his pock-marked face scowled in a mixture of anger and indecision. "Why are you here?"

"Car trouble." Grant grimaced and thumbed towards the track. "I'm stuck in a ditch back there." He eyed the foreman's rifle, a .30 calibre Remington, new and well oiled. "Out hunting, Carlos?"

"*Sim* . . . a deer," said Pereira curtly. He sucked his thin lips then glanced at his companions and nodded. As they lowered their guns he forced a smile. "Maybe you saw it, eh?"

"Sorry." Gaunt shook his head innocently. "Probably I frightened it off. A deer — I should have known." He paused and sighed realistically. "I saw lights moving up here and remembered those ghosts stories I'd heard. So I thought I'd take a look — and landed in that ditch instead. A pity about your deer, though."

"Another time will do." Pereira shrugged unemotionally. "Where is this car, senhor?"

"Not far." Gaunt paused hopefully. "You know, if you and your friends could spare a couple of minutes I'd be grateful. You see, I've got a bad back — the *medicos* won't let me lift anything heavy."

The Pension Board members, he decided, would probably have docked another twenty per cent off that pension if they'd seen him five minutes earlier. The hopeful smile still on his face, he waited.

Slowly, reluctantly, Pereira hitched his rifle by the sling over one shoulder and gestured to his companions. They followed Gaunt in silence to the track and along to where the Fiat lay ditched then, scowling, set to work while he watched and made apologetic noises about his back.

A few minutes heaving and struggling, occasionally broken by a curse, and the little car was finally manhandled clear. Cheerfully, Gaunt slapped the foreman on the back and beamed around.

"Obrigado, multo obrigado," he declared enthusiastically, reaching into his pocket. "Carlos, about that deer . . . "

"No matter." Pereira shook his head grimly. "But you might remember, senhor, that it is not wise to wander around these hills after dark." His lips tightened. "A man has been shot in mistake for a deer before now."

"It was damned stupid," agreed Gaunt, opening the car door. "I'll remember, believe me."

"Good." A wintery smile touched

Pereira's mouth. *"Boa noite,* Senhor Gaunt. There is a place where you can turn just a little way up."

Nodding, Gaunt climbed aboard, closed the door, and started the engine. As he set the Fiat moving, he gave the grim-faced trio a final wave.

The track widened enough to make a turn about fifty yards up. He brought the Fiat round then stopped for a moment, glancing at his watch.

He'd given Inez Torres almost fifteen minutes — and in the process got himself mobile again. Which was a reasonable enough success. Lighting a cigarette, well aware he was still being watched from the timber, he took a long draw on the tobacco and shivered, remembering the Remington.

A .30 calibre rifle had a muzzle velocity of 2200 feet per second, a muzzle energy of close on 2000 foot pounds. Which meant it punched a hole and kept on going. Or, as his old Parachute Regiment sergeant-instructor had loved to put it to the squad, "Just stand in line an' one shot will take care o' the damn lot of you."

Inez Torres and her brother had been lucky. He'd been equally lucky.

Now, he reckoned, it was time he found out exactly what he'd got into. Sergeant Manuel Costa's apparently wild-cat hunch about how Francis Preston had died suddenly seemed much less of a wisping whimsy than it had before — and that might be only a start.

Though that august and very practical civil servant, the Queen's and Lord Treasurer's Remembrancer, secure behind his desk in Edinburgh, might have taken the view that it was none of his department's damned business.

Gaunt shrugged. Edinburgh was a long way away. And if someone had murdered Preston then maybe the Remembrancer's external auditor should get involved — even if just to express annoyance.

The cigarette glowing between his lips, he set the Fiat trundling down the track again. When he passed the spot where the car had ditched the three men had gone.

But he'd a feeling they'd probably given up hunting that deer.

Stopped at the roadside with sidelights on and exhaust burbling, the red Lancia was waiting about a kilometre's distance outside Claras. Slowing the Fiat as he approached, seeing two shadowy figures aboard the coupé, Gaunt flicked his headlamps.

Inez Torres didn't waste time. Immediately he'd signalled, the Lancia's main beams were switched on and it pulled away, leaving him to follow.

They turned right at the first junction, and went roughly half a kilometre, then the Lancia signalled another turn and swung right again, this time into a narrow, tarmac road and from there into a short, gravelled drive lined with young, carefully spaced rose bushes. It led to a modest, hacienda-style bungalow and they stopped outside.

Switching off lights and engine, Jonathan Gaunt climbed out. The bungalow stood high above the twinkling lights of Claras, completely on its own, the only sound the faint rustle of the wind in the bushes.

The driver's door of the Lancia swung

open and Inez Torres emerged. Her coat and white trousers showed mud-stained in the moonlight, but her expression as Gaunt came over was one of genuine relief.

"I felt sick back there, just waiting," she said with a quiet sincerity. "It wasn't long — maybe only a minute, Senhor Gaunt. But I was afraid of what might have happened."

"I was counting on Sergeant Costa," said Gaunt with a mock solemnity. "He claims there's a law against shooting tourists out of season." He grinned at her, then his manner changed as he nodded towards the Lancia and the silent figure hunched in the front passenger seat. "Like some help?"

"It's all right now." She shook her head at the offer. "Luis knows we're home. I can manage."

Going round, she opened the other door. Her passenger left the car slowly, almost timidly, while she made soft encouraging noises and took his hand. Giving Gaunt a nervous glance, Luis Torres looked away again quickly and let his sister lead him towards the house.

Gaunt followed them quietly, waiting while the girl opened the front door and switched on a light.

He followed them in, closed the door, then, while Inez switched on other lights, stopped with something close to shock as he had his first full view of the strange, frail creature he'd helped rescue.

Luis Torres shared his sister's raven-black hair and fine-boned features. He was over medium height and cleanshaven and though his grey wool sweater and slacks were now muddy and torn they looked new and had cost money.

But his face was thin, parchment pale and child-like in its expression. Dark eyes stared at Gaunt with a puzzled, struggling emptiness while he rubbed his bony hands nervously, one against the other. It was like looking at the shrunken, helpless husk of a man who had been drained both physically and mentally.

Shrunken and helpless — Gaunt felt shock give way to pity, then Inez Torres came back.

"I'll get Luis to bed," she said with a forced cheerfulness then gestured towards one of the lighted rooms. "Help yourself to a drink in there. I won't be long. Luis . . . " she turned, holding out a hand.

Her brother took it, gave Gaunt another puzzled, empty look, and went away with her.

Gaunt entered the room. It had a polished wood floor with sheepskin scatter rugs and had been furnished in a modern, almost Scandinavian style. A long bookcase and a professional stereo tape and record player unit shared most of one wall, a natural stone fireplace with a copper hood occupied the main area on the opposite side. But the really eye-catching feature was a full-length portrait in oils, life-size, of Inez Torres in the traditional black dress of a *fadista* singer.

Whoever had created the portrait had tried for a conventional dramatic presentation, complete with a background of velvet drapes. But he'd caught something else in the process, a face with a special, compelling quality of warmth and zest for life. A quality that so far Gaunt had only glimpsed briefly and occasionally in the original.

There was a small cocktail bar in a corner. Going there, he poured himself a full three fingers of whisky and this time he didn't add water. He took a long swallow and sighed appreciatively as the liquor soothed and tingled its way down, drowning a tiredness which had been creeping in on him now that the excitement had ended.

Carrying the glass, Gaunt went over to the stereo unit and thumbed through some of the records lying beside it. Most were *fado* discs, a few with Inez Torres' name on the label. Others were modern jazz and a couple of Frank Sinatra oldies, well worn.

Leaving them, he stopped at the bookcase, puzzled. One shelf held manuals on car maintenance, another was half-filled with electronics textbooks. Even allowing for the novels and travel books which made up the rest, it was a collection which didn't match the positive feminine personality responsible for the rest of the room.

Going back to the portrait again, studying the vibrant mood and beauty caught by the brush and canvas, he heard footsteps and turned.

"He's sleeping already," said Inez Torres, coming into the room. "He was exhausted — and right now I feel that way too."

She had removed her coat and changed shoes for soft, open-backed slippers. Going over to the bar, she poured herself a drink, very deliberately added a couple of ice cubes, swirled them in the glass, tasted the result, then sat wearily on a cushioned stool beside the fireplace and looked up at him.

"I haven't thanked you yet," she said quietly.

"No need." Gaunt shook his head. "Inez, how long has he been that way?"

"About two years — there was a car crash, a bad one." She shivered a little, bent, switched on an electric fire in the hearth, and watched it begin to glow. "The *medicos* said he would die. He didn't, not the way they meant."

"Brain damage?"

She nodded. "They say Luis has a mental age of about four. Some still hope there's a chance he'll improve — but only a chance." Looking up, she continued to

102

shut all emotion from her voice. "Before it happened, he was very different — a lieutenant in the navy, big brother."

"I'm sorry." Gaunt meant it, understanding more than she could realise. "It can't be easy."

"I can afford help, a woman who was a nurse. But I give her time off when I'm not working, like tonight." Inez Torres sipped her drink again and shrugged. "I thought it would be all right to leave him alone while I went to see Manuel Costa — but it was a mistake. He'd gone when I got back here."

She took the cigarette Gaunt offered. He lit it for her, took another for himself, then stood with his back to the fire.

"Still, you knew where to find him," he mused. "Was that just luck?"

"I looked in several places." A sudden caution showed on her face then had gone, but stayed in a careful choice of words. "Luis thinks like a child, goes to places he knew as a child . . . "

"And can get lost or frightened the same way." Gaunt nodded and drew on his cigarette. "I said it before — it can't he easy. Was it some problem about Luis that took you over to Sergeant Costa?"

"No." She shook her head quickly. "I — that was another matter, a private matter."

"I wondered, that's all," soothed Gaunt. "Does he often wander off?"

"Hardly ever." Her eyes showed a gathering anger. "Even when he does, he wouldn't harm anyone — I told you, he's like a child."

"That's what I meant," said Gaunt grimly. "I still saw three armed men hunting him like an animal. If they'd caught him . . . " he stopped and shrugged. "I think Sergeant Costa would like to hear about it. And that he'd have all three of them in the local jail within an hour."

Waiting, he took another drink of whisky and watched her, already guessing what was coming.

"No." She bit her lip. "I — I don't want trouble. Not when it might involve Luis. Perhaps later — or if I see Doctor Sollas . . . " she paused helplessly " . . . but not now, please."

"If that's how you want it." Gaunt set down his glass and nodded, his face devoid of expression. "Thanks for the drink. I'll get on my way."

"There's no hurry." She rose quickly, flushing. "I didn't mean . . ."

"I hoped you didn't." Gaunt smiled at her. "You know, I'm here for a couple more days anyway, and I won't be working all the time. When I've the chance, how about helping me to be a tourist for a few hours?"

"All right." She managed an answering smile. "But I have to work in the evenings."

Gaunt nodded. "And I'm getting a conducted tour round the digging site tomorrow morning. How about the afternoon?"

"I'll be ready." The smile came more easily, then she had a new thought — or one she'd saved. "Before you go, let me show you something."

Curious, he went out with her into the hall and deeper into the house. She stopped at a half-opened door and beckoned him nearer. Standing beside the girl, her warmth close and tantalising, he looked and understood.

A small night-light burned beside a

single bed, throwing a glow over Luis Torres's sleeping figure. He was breathing gently, the thin, pale face relaxed and peaceful, and suddenly it wasn't too hard to imagine how he'd once been.

The room was a man's room, with photographs of naval vessels on the walls and an electric razor lying on the dressing table. But a child's jigsaw puzzle was on the floor beside the bed, abandoned half completed.

Gently, with a sudden compassion, Gaunt laid a hand on Inez Torres's arm and drew her away. She said nothing till they were at the front door of the house then, as Gaunt opened it, she moistened her lips.

"Can you really imagine him harming anyone?" she asked almost bitterly.

"No." He didn't know if it was a lie or not. There were other questions he wanted to ask her, about Francis Preston, about the digging site, about what had happened after the funeral. But they would have to wait. "Inez, do one thing for me. Have a talk with Sergeant Costa, as a friend."

"Perhaps." She looked out into the

night, where the sky now sparkled with stars. "Let me think about it. And — and you?"

"It's not my business — I'll say nothing."

"Thank you," she said, openly relieved. *"Boa noite* . . . good night, Senhor Gaunt."

"People call me Jonathan."

"Jonathan. I'll remember." She smiled almost shyly as he went out, then the door closed gently behind him.

★ ★ ★

It was after midnight when he parked the Fiat outside the Hotel Da Gama. The spotlight on the fountain in the square had been switched off and the houses around were in darkness. Claras apparently had an early to bed, early to rise philosophy, whatever its inhabitants did with their day.

The briefcase under one arm, Gaunt found the hotel door unlocked. Inside, a light was still burning over the reception desk and beneath the light, white jacket unbuttoned and head lolling, Jaime was dozing in a chair. Quietly passing the young porter, Gaunt reached the stairs and started up towards his room.

A board creaked underfoot and he heard a yawn.

"*Chame*, Senhor Gaunt?" asked Jaime from below, pausing for another yawn. "Would you like a call in the morning?"

"I suppose so." Stopping, he looked back and nodded. "Make it for eight o'clock."

"*Oito horas* — okay." Jaime chalked the time on a slate then grinned up again. "I was waiting here to see you, senhor."

"So you could report back to Sergeant Costa?" suggested Gaunt acidly. "Keep up with the market, laddie. You've been wasting your time — ask Costa."

"I did." Jaime grimaced at the reminder. "But there was another reason — one that might interest you. At least, I think so."

Gaunt raised an eyebrow then came back down a couple of steps.

"Well?"

Sadly, Jaime spread his hands. Digging into his pocket, Gaunt flicked a five escudo piece towards the desk. It was caught smartly in mid-air and vanished.

"A man from the digging camp came here maybe half an hour ago," said the youngster, grinning. "He was most anxious to know if you were back in the hotel. His name is Alfred — I have seen him in the bar before."

Gaunt frowned. "What did you tell him?"

"What I thought you might want, that you had just gone to bed." Jaime paused and winked. "He too gave me five escudos — I was to say nothing."

"How long till you buy your own hotel?" asked Gaunt bleakly.

The brown, cherubic face wrinkled in a serious frown. "I reckon five, maybe six years. But it will be nearer Estoril, where the money is."

Gaunt sighed and leaned on the banister, considering the sharp-eyed gaze which met his own.

"I'll bet on you making it — unless you land in jail first," he agreed with conviction. "And here's a chance to make a bonus ten escudos towards it. What kind of grudge would make anyone start throwing bricks at the mourners after Senhor Preston's funeral? I want an answer, Jaime, otherwise I'm going to come down and belt you around the ears till I get one."

The boy started to grin, then saw his expression and had a change of mind.

"People liked Senhor Preston," he said cautiously. "If we — if they hadn't liked him, it wouldn't have mattered."

"What wouldn't have mattered?" Gaunt came down another step in menacing style. "No riddles, Jaime. I'm too tired for them."

"Okay — okay, Senhor Gaunt." Jaime swallowed hard and nodded. "Then maybe it was because those men he worked with laugh about how he died — that he was drunk when he fell into that trench." His young mouth tightened with a surprising anger and contempt. "Sure, Senhor Preston drank a lot. An' sometimes he looked like he should be poured back into a bottle. But not that night."

"What makes you so sure?"

"Because he stopped here for a drink late on — one glass of brandy, no more."

He saw the doubt on Gaunt's face and gestured emphatically with both hands. "It is the truth — I even served him myself."

"Does Sergeant Costa know?"

"He did not ask. I only tell him what he asks," was the sullen reply. "Why do more?"

"That's your business." Gaunt rubbed a hand along his chin, feeling the rasp of the day's stubble. "Was Preston alone?"

"*Sim*, when he came an' when he left. All he said was he'd been in Lisbon — but he was angry about something."

The story had a ring of truth. Nodding, Gaunt reached for his pocket.

"No — not this time." Jaime stopped him with a head-shake. "For Senhor Preston, make it what you call 'on the house' — okay?"

"On the house," agreed Gaunt softly. "Thanks, Jaime."

Leaving the boy, he went up to his room. He found the bed had been turned down and the balcony window closed with the curtains shut. Otherwise, everything seemed as he'd left it.

Or almost everything. Going over to

the dressing table, he checked the drawers and smiled. Someone had been rummaging through them, someone not as neat or experienced as Sergeant Costa.

But nothing was missing. Maybe Jaime left that till later.

He undressed slowly, his back aching from the sheer fatigue of a long, long day. Still — he brightened, remembering how he'd carried Luis Torres at a run across that slope. He'd managed it.

Maybe because he hadn't had time to wonder if he could.

Finding the painkiller tablets, he swallowed a couple before he slid naked between the cool, white sheets. Then he lay thinking. About Luis Torres and where he'd been the night Francis Preston had died. About Inez Torres and Preston — then, irrelevantly, about the stock market back in Britain and his brewery shares.

But when sleep came he dreamed of being hunted through a strange, nightmare labyrinth by awesome, giant half-man, half-beast figures.

The kind of nightmare a child might have.

★ ★ ★

He woke to the swish of curtains being drawn and sunlight pouring into the darkened room. A plump, busty hotel maid finished the task then turned, looked at him with widening eyes, and giggled before she made a swift retreat from the room.

Yawning and puzzled, Gaunt propped himself up on his elbows and saw he'd kicked off the sheets sometime during the night. He grinned at his naked body, thinking it might have been more of a compliment if she'd made another kind of noise, then yawned again and got up.

There was a coffee and rolls breakfast on a tray beside the bed and outside the window the sky was bright blue. The coffee pot was blistering hot to the touch so he shaved and dressed first, choosing a dark blue shirt and matching slacks, topping them with an oatmeal sports coat, and laying out a dark red tie. Then, once he'd eaten, he lit a cigarette, stuffed the tie in a pocket, and left.

The same hotel maid was busy with a vacuum cleaner in the downstairs lobby. He winked at her and heard another giggle as he went out.

Claras was already wide awake. Farm trucks were tumbling through the square and a row of makeshift market stalls had sprung up around the fountain, their owners carefully arranging displays of fish and vegetables, used clothing, salvaged auto parts and anything else likely to find a buyer. There was no sign of the knitted lace, carved wood or metalwork of the *artigos regionais* variety . . . the souvenir stallowners made their killing in the season and were probably holidaying in the South of France on the proceeds.

Flicking away his cigarette stub, Gaunt headed over to where he'd left the Fiat, then slowed his pace and gave a wry grin. Sergeant Costa was already there, wearing his sunglasses and a shirt even more dazzling than its predecessor but with a far from happy expression on his lean, leathery features as he considered the car's crumpled bodywork.

"Good morning," said Gaunt warily. "I — ah — went into a ditch."

"Bom dia." Manuel Costa returned the greeting gloomily. "I heard, Senhor Gaunt — in detail."

Gaunt nodded, rubbing a hand along the bent metal. It dislodged a heavy flaking of paint in a way that made Costa wince.

"From Inez?" he asked.

"Partly." Costa brought the sunglasses lower on his nose with a forefinger and eyed Gaunt oddly over their rims. "But the rest came from Doctor Sollas. He telephoned us late last night, reporting a new incident at the digging site. It — ah — seems three of his brave labour squad might well have caught an armed intruder if a certain damned fool Englishman . . ."

"I'm from Scotland."

"Muito obrigado." The policeman gave a nod of mock solemnity. "If this damned fool Scotchman visitor had not come blundering in, I can tell you the good doctor is not amused." His thin lips tightened. "On the other hand Inez Torres also telephoned me, but unofficially. I'm glad you were there, Senhor Gaunt — if my brother-in-law

115

asks you to pay for the damage, tell him to go to hell."

"Thanks." Gaunt propped himself against the Fiat's roof and looked out at the busy square. "What can you do about it, Sergeant?"

"Nothing — or the next best thing," said Costa wearily. "She refuses to make an official complaint."

"In case it comes out her brother might have killed Preston?" asked Gaunt in a mild voice.

"She told you that?" Manuel Costa's mouth fell open.

"No," admitted Gaunt. "But I think it's there."

Costa sighed, then forced a smile and an answering wave as a truck driver leaned out of his cab and shouted a greeting. He switched to a scowl as the truck rumbled on.

"Then it's a damn fool idea," he said with sour irritation. "Don't blame me for it. I know Luis — and he liked Preston." He paused, sucking his teeth. "Still, it explains why she came to see me yesterday, with a crazy story about being worried in case their house was ever burgled — we have had some burglaries lately, petty things, probably two men involved. Still, Inez isn't the nervous kind and — yes, she asked a lot about Preston and how he died."

"And?"

Costa grimaced. "She is a friend. Maybe I hinted a little more than I should, which wouldn't help. But — no, not Luis. He wouldn't hurt a fly."

"Even if the fly frightened him?" Gaunt drew a finger along the Fiat's dusty metal and examined the result. "You can't hide from that, Sergeant."

"No." Costa gave a reluctant scowl.

"And we don't know how often Luis manages to sneak out of that house at night . . . "

Costa swore. "I said Preston was his friend. That was why Preston saw Inez so often, not the other way round. He would spend hours with Luis, showing him puzzles, games — trying to make his mind work." A bitter smile twisted across his thin face. "Preston said all *medicos* were failed garage mechanics, that the mind was just another machine to be repaired."

It rang true to Francis Preston's character. Nodding, Gaunt let an old tractor go by in a noisy stench of exhaust fumes then asked a question that had been puzzling him.

"Aren't there other relatives?"

"Didn't she tell you?" Costa eyed the departing tractor bleakly, the exhaust cloud still belching. "Luis had two passengers when he crashed, their mother and father. They were killed. Until then" — he sighed — "most people envied Luis. He was good-looking, popular, that navy uniform brought the girls swarming around — though he was an electronics specialist, the kind of sailor too important to send out to sea. Now — well, you've seen him."

"But you've still got that hunch about Preston," mused Gaunt. "Maybe it's contagious, Sergeant — and there are other possibilities."

"Of course." Costa brightened.

"What did the post-mortem report say about liquor?"

"That there wasn't enough to be significant." Costa frowned. "*Porque* . . . why?"

"Jaime said the same — Preston stopped at the Da Gama on his way back from Lisbon. He was alone then."

Costa muttered under his breath. "I wasn't told that."

"He says you didn't ask," grinned Gaunt. "But it doesn't help much. What about the people he visited in Lisbon?"

"I have a list." Manuel Costa looked worried. "They were only asked when he left to come back here. But for the police to ask them questions again would mean giving reasons. Unless . . . " He paused hopefully.

"I could look up a couple." Gaunt saw Costa's delight and added a warning. "But remember, I've got my own interests. They come first."

"All I want is one hard fact," said Costa fervently. "Get me that, from anywhere, one my superiors can't ignore and . . . "

He stopped, frowning, as a car horn beeped almost beside them. The car drew in, Georges Salvador's blue Jaguar with the plump, sallow-faced owner at the wheel.

"Sollas's landlord," murmured Gaunt

as Salvador beckoned him over. "I'll be back."

He heard Costa grunt as he left. The sound was far from polite.

"Senhor Gaunt." Salvador greeted him with a white-toothed smile as he reached the car. "How are you after last night's experience?"

"On the hill?" Gaunt grinned. "Fine — but news seems to travel fast."

"I heard from Doctor Sollas. He had to telephone me this morning — it was about a detail in the lease for the villa." Salvador chuckled and ran a hand along the car's leather-rimmed steering wheel. "Well, now you have more respect for our ditches, eh?"

"A lot more," said Gaunt dryly. "How did things go at the casino last night?"

"Win a little, lose a little — my usual. Though my friends were less fortunate." Salvador eyed him keenly. "Will you be here long enough to try your own luck?"

"There's that chance," agreed Gaunt vaguely. "If I save hard, I might manage to play a fruit machine or two."

"If you do, be my guest — just

let me know." Salvador blipped the accelerator lightly. "Arrangements could be made, discreetly, of course. I know your position."

"Thanks." Gaunt nodded neutrally. "On your way to see Sollas?"

"No, I have another little interest to attend to." Salvador blipped the accelerator again. "Anyway, take care. And remember what I said."

Gaunt stood back as the blue car purred away. It had disappeared round a corner before he got back to Manuel Costa.

"I've had an offer," he said dryly. "A free night at the casino."

Costa's nostrils twitched in disgust. "Will you go?"

"That depends what he's selling," mused Gaunt. "You don't like him?"

"Me?" Costa grimaced. "As a humble sergeant of detectives . . . " He stopped and gestured his disgust. "Jesu, no, I don't like a man who makes money so easily."

"Meaning?"

"He plays the stock market in Lisbon. Reads a few newspapers in bed, makes a few phone calls — what kind of a man would call that a day's work?"

"Jealousy, Sergeant," murmured Gaunt. "It's not so easy, believe me. I've tried but never got far."

"My heart bleeds," said Costa cynically, giving the Fiat's nearest tyre an experimental kick. "I'll leave those names for you at the Da Gama. Have a good day — and don't fall down any holes, eh?"

Whistling a tune, he ambled away.

4

MOONLIGHT might satisfy song writers, but daytime brought its own compensations as Jonathan Gaunt motored the hill route to the Castelo de Rosa digging site. Where the Fiat had ditched on a nightmare-edged track was now a pleasant, jolting but uneventful drive through a leafy lane. Pine and poplars, tall and majestic, cast their shade and were punctuated here and there by an occasional, isolated patch of bulky, ancient cork trees.

When he cleared the trees, the old Moorish watchtower stood like a cool, austere sentinel dominating the little valley ahead. A simple, geometrically precise structure, slab-sided, the upper section's tumbled, broken walls telling of some past calamity, it was built of a coral-hued stone which seemed to glow in the rays of the sun.

Gaunt stopped the car for a moment, remembering land-marks from the night before — and seeing them in a new perspective.

The scrub bushland where Luis Torres had been so relentlessly hunted had become a dark green patchwork of shrubbery set in a rich, pastel carpet of long grass and delicate wild flowers, splashed here and there by a yellow blaze of myrtle. On either side of the clearing the timber began again. But not as thickly as he'd imagined and starting a lot further back than he'd realised.

Wryly aware of the way his luck had held, Gaunt switched his attention to the digging site. Broad brown furrows of earth, marking trench excavations, radiated out from the watch-tower's base to join other, narrower furrows which traced an outline like the pencilled shape of the Roman villa he'd seen on Arthur Sollas's map. A few small figures were moving around the trenches and there were cars parked beside the two wooden huts which seemed to form the team's base.

But the fence interested him too. Built of high mesh wire laced to concrete poles, it surrounded a long, oval area which contained the Castelo trenches and a lot more — he guessed the total at some four acres of ground. And, like a stopper in a bottle, it blocked the route of the track winding through the middle of the clearing.

Open, the track was a gateway to the high, wooded hills beyond as it had probably been for centuries, perhaps even back to a time when the watch-tower had been built to guard it.

Closed, it was the kind of irritation any peasant farmer wanting to get to shops or market would find hard to tolerate. Even when the reasons were known to have firm official backing.

But for the moment how the locals felt was among the least of his worries. Releasing the handbrake, Gaunt flicked the Fiat into gear and let it trickle on.

He'd been seen. As the car neared the site gate a workman hurried from the direction of the huts and swung the gate open, waving him through and pointing over to where the other cars were parked. Gaunt stopped beside them and climbed out, his mouth shaping a greeting as he saw Arthur Sollas striding towards him from the nearest hut.

"So you made it this time." Sollas was wearing old baseball boots, a grubby khaki shirt and shorts which emphasised his paunch. The bulky figure stopped a few paces away and eyed Gaunt stonily. "What the hell was your idea last night?"

Gaunt grimaced apologetically. "I saw lights and got curious."

"Curious?" Sollas grunted the word. "You could have wrecked that car — and you might have got your head blown off."

"The deer hunters?" Gaunt showed innocent surprise. "I was glad enough to see them."

"Maybe, but they weren't after deer — Pereira didn't want to alarm you." Sollas hesitated, rubbing the scar on his nose. "We had a prowler. So — well, they went out to scare him off."

"They'd enough firepower," mused Gaunt.

Sollas nodded. "Pereira says they're pretty certain he had a shotgun. Anyway, he got away — and now you're here, we might as well get started on the guided tour." He gave a cynical grimace.

"Unless you want to wait for Marsh and his wife — they're coming over."

"No thanks." He could do without meeting Francis Preston's relatives again unless it became essential — and he hoped it wouldn't. "How did they make out last night?"

"If they'd found anything you'd have heard." Sollas booted a stray pebble almost viciously. "Bernie Ryan looked in after midnight and found them ripping the lining out of Preston's jacket — and they're still trying. That's why they're coming here." He scowled out across the site for a moment then shrugged. "Well, let's begin at the beginning, the watch-tower."

Gaunt followed him and they tramped along a narrow wooden boardwalk which spanned its way across the nearest trenches. Here and there Gaunt caught a glimpse of exposed patches of broken mosaic flooring down below and once Sollas thumbed towards the butt edge of a fragment of wall which had a triangulation mark chalked across its face.

"These were early stage probings."

Sollas stopped as they reached the tower and gestured back. "We were lucky we got the proof we were right almost first go, only about five feet down, though we had to go a lot deeper later."

"All because of this." Gaunt felt dwarfed beneath the weathered pink-hued stonework. He rubbed a hand over its rough texture. "What made it so special to Preston?"

"The stonework was obviously quarried, but all different sized blocks pieced together like a jigsaw — he reckoned they'd been salvaged from something a lot bigger." Sollas sucked his teeth in mournful admiration. "As usual, he guessed right — almost right, anyway."

Going over to a gaping archway, Gaunt looked inside the tower. It was shadowed, weed-choked, and smelled of mildewed decay. A crumbling stone stairway led up to the next floor but was blocked halfway where a small tree sprouted from a crack, its long, thin branches reaching almost hungrily towards a few rays of sunlight filtering down from somewhere above.

"Well?" demanded Sollas. "What do you think of it?"

Gaunt shook his head. "It's not my line, Doctor. If I was asked, I'd probably slap a demolition order on it."

"At least you're honest." Sollas chuckled almost amiably. "That's half the trouble. Today's slum can be tomorrow's treasure-house. Like to see more?"

"Yes." Gaunt cleared his throat diplomatically. "How about where the accident happened?"

Sighing, Arthur Sollas nodded and led the way again. They went back the way they'd come and along more boardwalk, skirting trenches which gradually deepened and widened, their loose earth often supported by timber and corrugated iron shuttering. In one, Gaunt glimpsed two workmen slowly and carefully scraping away earth from an emerging stone bench. In another, a man with a hand trowel was down on his knees cleaning a patch of mosaic flooring.

"Down here," said Sollas curtly, stopping and matching action to words by clambering down a runged ladder.

Gaunt followed him. The trench was about twelve feet below ground level, just wide enough to let two men stand side by side, and supported by piling and corrugated sheeting. A stretch of plain stone paving underfoot ended in a mixture of clay and rubble, and a few paces beyond, where there were signs of experimental cuttings into the sides of the trench, it all ended in a caved-in mess of soil, collapsed timber and twisted sheeting.

"We dug him out from under there." Arthur Sollas stuck his hands in the pockets of his shorts and scowled, his booming voice a full tone grimmer. "You see what happened before — we ran out beyond the Roman villa's boundaries. But Preston took convincing before he'd agree we stopped."

"Because it meant defeat for him?"

"That's how he saw it." Sollas stopped and turned as a voice hailed him from up above. One of the workmen beamed down hopefully at them. Sighing, Sollas waved a hand then turned to Gaunt. "A problem — wait here and I'll be back."

Gaunt watched him climb up the ladder and disappear. Then, lighting a cigarette, he went closer to the collapsed tangle of debris and considered it with some care. Rain-soaked, waterlogged soil and loosened timbers — it wouldn't have taken much to bring the lot down. If Francis Preston had come this way after dark at the whim of some stubborn devil of impulse, a stumble against one of those timbers might have been enough.

But the word was still only 'might'.

Shrugging, ready to turn away, he saw something glint just clear of the fall. It was a tiny piece of broken glass, thin and curved. Puzzled, he stooped and saw other, small fragments — the remains of a broken watch-glass.

On impulse, he gathered a few of the pieces in his handkerchief then rose thoughtfully. Carlos Pereira hadn't been wearing a wrist-watch — but the mark of a strap had been there on his left wrist.

A grunt from above brought him round as Arthur Sollas began coming back down the ladder. Gaunt quickly stuffed the handkerchief back in his pocket and tried hard to slip back into his role of interested bystander.

"False alarm," said Sollas, as he reached the bottom of the trench and came over. "Someone found a chunk of kitchen pottery — not worth a damn, but they know we pay a bonus for anything worth while so they always come running." He chuckled and looked around. "Gaunt, if you know your history you don't need me to tell you these Romans were sophisticated people. We've found traces of warm-air central heating, a heated bath, even piped water and drainage — things the world lost afterwards and had to invent again. I'd say whoever lived here was important, maybe even a provincial governor."

"Then what went wrong?" Gaunt relaxed, deciding the man hadn't spotted what he'd done.

"Fire and sword — I'll show you." Beckoning, Sollas set off down the trench. They joined another, not as deep but wider, then followed it round an angle.

On the other side the way was partly blocked by a heavy stone pillar, ornately carved but broken in the middle like a stick of seaside rock. The top section lay against one side of the trench, and the digging team had jammed in a couple of struts of timber to hold it in position.

"Careful now" — the big man squeezed

past, waited till Gaunt joined him, then pointed — "in there."

A narrow archway in an unexpected wall formed the entrance to a small, cell-like room and there was light inside. Stooping, Gaunt went in, saw Martin Lawson squatting on the sandy floor, nodded as the fat archaeologist beamed a greeting — then stopped and blinked.

Lawson was hunched down beside a row of five yellowed, fragile human skeletons. He'd been clearing sand and grit from the nearest with a small paintbrush.

"Good, aren't they?" said Lawson happily. Reaching over, he dragged a kerosene lamp closer and sat back on his heels, wiping a hand across his bald head. "We don't find this kind of thing often, Gaunt. But when that pillar fell outside it sealed the door — a real stroke of luck."

Two of the skeletons had shattered skulls. Beaming, Lawson used the paintbrush to point to a blackened metal spearhead still jammed in the breastbone of another.

"Fire and sword, like I said," rumbled

Arthur Sollas, squeezing in beside them.

"No doubt about it," declared Lawson enthusiastically. "Almost certainly the villa was attacked in some local uprising. These would be early Roman casualities, killed and brought down here. Then, later, there was a final storming — the entire household slaughtered, bodies stripped and plundered . . . "

"Don't make a meal of it, Martin," said Sollas wearily. "He can imagine the rest."

Gaunt nodded and shivered a little without knowing why. Sollas noticed and grinned a little.

"If you've seen enough . . . " He nodded towards the archway.

Thankfully, Gaunt eased back out into the open and stood upright. He heard Arthur Sollas grunting a way through behind him, glanced back — then sensed as much as heard a strange, soft, almost groaning noise. Out of the corner of his eye he caught a movement at the top of the trench.

Then the great carved stone pillar was falling towards him, one of its wooden supports splintering with a crackle, dirt and gravel fogging the air.

For a moment he was paralysed then he threw himself straight backward, smashing into Sollas, sending the big man reeling, then bringing his hands up over his head in a final futility of protection.

The pillar wasn't falling straight. An edge caught the opposite wall of the trench, it twisted — then landed with a reverberating crash on the stone slabs inches from his feet. For a moment more the air was filled with dust and the noise of trickling earth and gravel.

Then there was silence. Absolute, total silence — till Arthur Sollas pushed and cursed his way out of the little cell. He stared at the fallen pillar then at Gaunt, who was leaning shakily against the wall, and shook his head in something close to stunned disbelief.

"You all right?" he demanded finally.

Gaunt nodded. There was a deep indentation in the corrugated iron shuttering where the pillar had struck. The flagstones at his feet were shattered. If he hadn't dived back, if the pillar had fallen fractionally straighter — then he'd be dead, a smashed, bloodied smear for Sergeant Costa to theorise around.

"How the hell did it happen?" Scowling, red-faced, Arthur Sollas glared around, then focussed his rage. "Carlos, get down here, damn you!"

The foreman was peering at them from the lip of the trench, his swarthy face sickly, his eyes fixed unbelievingly on Gaunt.

"Did you hear me?" rasped Sollas.

"*Sim* . . . yes, Doctor. *Immediatamente!*" Carlos Pereira scrambled away.

As he vanished, Martin Lawson squeezed out into the open from the archway and blinked like a plump, confused dormouse as he saw the pillar.

"Is — is it damaged?" he asked weakly. "Ah — are you hurt, Gaunt?"

"No." Gaunt managed a grin. "And I'll try to catch it for you next time."

"Damn the damage," snarled Sollas. "And stay out of this, Martin. Get back to your blasted boneyard."

Lawson shrank back, shaking his head. Hands on hips, legs apart, Sollas switched viciously as Pereira hurried towards them along the trench from some nearby ladder.

"Well?" grated Sollas, his nostrils flaring. "Didn't I tell you this blasted pillar was to be made secure?"

Moistening his lips, Pereira fidgeted a moment then nodded.

"Then how the hell did this happen?"

The man spread his hands vaguely and tried a nervously apologetic grin. "I don't know, Doctor Sollas. Maybe Senhor Gaunt . . . "

"Senhor Gaunt did damn all. The thing just fell." Two strides took Sollas to the foreman, two massive fists grabbed him by the shirt and nearly dragged him off his feet. "Now you'll fix it this time. *Pressa* . . . right now, understand?"

Nodding quickly, Pereira looked relieved as Sollas relaxed his grip. Then he turned to Gaunt, forcing the same sickly grin.

"Accidents happen, Senhor Gaunt. I am sorry."

Gaunt shrugged. "I'm still in one piece, Carlos. Luckier than Senhor Preston, eh?" He paused, then grimaced as he added, "I suppose you helped dig him out?"

"*Nao, senhor* . . . not me.*" Pereira shook his head quickly and glanced sideways at Arthur Sollas. "I — uh — was in Estoril that night. I did not get back till much later."

"He's got a woman there," said Sollas wearily. "Get on with it, man."

Nodding Pereira turned away and began shouting orders to some of the other workmen who were now gathered above.

"Tour's over," said Sollas bleakly. "Gaunt, you look like you could use a drink."

"And I feel like I look," agreed Gaunt fervently.

They left Lawson still making tutting noises over the fallen pillar and went along to where they could climb out of the trench. From there, Sollas steered a direct course towards the huts near the gate and led the way into the larger of the two, which was laid out as an office.

"Enjoy your tour?" greeted Bernie Ryan, grinning up at Gaunt from behind a desk made of old packing-cases. Without waiting for an answer, he switched his grin towards Sollas. "What was the excitement? Have some more of your early Roman chamber-pots turned up, Doc?"

"No." Sollas went straight to a locked cupboard, produced a key, and opened the door. "We damned nearly had a second body on our hands."

Raising an eyebrow, the white-haired photographer gave a startled whistle.

"How?" he demanded.

They told him, while Sollas brought three tumblers and a brandy bottle from the cupboard and splashed a stiff measure of brandy into each tumbler.

"God give us all patience." Ryan rubbed his chin appreciatively as the story ended, then neatly caught the drink that slid across the desk top towards him. "Gaunt, between this and last night, I'd hate like hell to be your insurance company." He raised the glass in a general toast, sipped, then said with a total irrelevance, "The locals have a neat name for a drink before noon, a *matobicho* . . . a germ-killer. See some of their sanitation and you'll know why." Stopping, he frowned. "Hey, where's Martin? He can usually smell a drink being poured at half-mile range."

"Still talking to his skeletons," answered Sollas.

"An appreciative audience at last," declared Ryan solemnly. He gestured around. "Well, here's where the real work is done, Gaunt. See and admire — it's time somebody did."

Gaunt grinned. The timber walls were covered in pinned-up photographs of the excavation area, some of them general views and others close-up studies of pottery ornaments, fragments of statuary or rusted sword blades. But the only trace of the originals he could see was an elaborate mosaic tile which Ryan had as a drink mat.

He asked why.

"Most of it goes straight into a crate and off to the museum people in Lisbon — another of their rules." Arthur Sollas slumped heavily into a camp-chair and shrugged. "Not that we're worried. The real prize here has been just finding the place."

"And what happens when you leave?" asked Gaunt.

Sollas frowned. "That's been agreed.

There's one small section which will stay fenced off and private — for another year. The Romans weren't necessarily the first people here and I'd like to try going deeper. But that depends on backers and money. The rest is handed back to the Portuguese authorities and they'll probably open it as a tourist attraction. Lawson's boneyard should bring them running."

"Don't knock the tourists," murmured Ryan lazily. "They could be bread-and-butter to an out-of-work photographer. Maybe I'll stay on and earn the odd escudo as a guide or something." He swung his feet up on the desk top and grinned at Gaunt. "It's that or a share of the Treasure Trove reward money you're waving around."

"It's there," mused Grant. "Somebody's going to earn it."

"But not me." Ryan grimaced. "And not Marsh and his wife, if there's any justice. When are they due here anyway, Doc?"

"About eleven. Any time now," answered Sollas shortly.

"My cue to leave," said Gaunt with a

grin. He finished his drink and laid down the glass. "I'll be in touch."

"Just take care, then," advised Ryan without moving. "Third time might not be so lucky."

Gaunt had already thought of that. He said goodbye, left the hut, and was over at the Fiat when he heard a shout and turned.

A camera clicked. Standing in the hut doorway, Ryan took a second shot then lowered the camera.

"One for the visitors' book," he called. "Order your copies now."

Gaunt grinned, got into the Fiat, and set it moving. Then, as he neared the gate in the fence, he slowed again. Pereira was there, standing bleak-faced and talking earnestly to another of the workmen. Stopping beside them Gaunt wound down his window and beckoned the foreman over.

"Forget about that business with the pillar, Carlos," he said easily. "Accidents happen."

"*Obrigado*, Senhor Gaunt." Pereira nodded gloomily. "You are going now?"

"Back to Claras, to meet someone."

Gaunt eyed him innocently. "I said I'd be there before noon. What time do you make it?"

The man hesitated then shook his head. "I don't have a watch, Senhor Gaunt."

"I just wondered — mine is misbehaving." Gaunt raised a hand in farewell and set the Fiat moving again. Another workman opened the gate and he drove through without a backward glance.

But one shove from above would have been enough to send that pillar crashing down. Pereira had tried to kill him in the trench. Kill him or at very least frighten him off.

Exactly why didn't matter. It was personal now, and the little fragments of glass nestling in his handkerchief might prove very interesting to a certain humble sergeant of detectives.

★ ★ ★

A leisurely ten minute drive brought him back to Claras. He left the Fiat in the square near the fountain and was walking over to the hotel when two determined

143

figures hurried from a shop doorway to intercept him. John and Sarah Marsh looked tired-eyed and pasty-faced in the bright sunlight, but they greeted him with a resolute purpose.

"Gaunt, we're going to stay on an extra couple of days," said Marsh without preamble. "I'm damned if we want to, but with the kind of money you're offering we can't take chances."

Sarah Marsh nodded. She had a paper carrier bag in one hand, bulging with small parcels.

"Including whether somebody here isn't hiding more of Uncle Frank's stuff, just waiting till we've gone," she said grimly.

"Somebody — or anyone in particular?" asked Gaunt.

Husband and wife exchanged a glance then Sarah Marsh sniffed. "Well, there's Doctor Sollas for a start. He — he's the kind that might. Big and noisy but probably desperate for money."

"Aren't we all?" Gaunt sighed sympathetically. "I thought you were visiting this morning, both of you."

"We are." John Marsh flicked a strand

of his long, mousey hair back from his forehead and brightened a little. "That photographer character Ryan says he thinks there's maybe some of Uncle Frank's notebooks and papers still out there."

"So we'll find out," said Sarah Marsh. She stabbed an indignant forefinger. "But if any of them are trying a fast one on us . . ."

She left the threat unfinished. Her husband nodded.

"The other thing we've done is cable the solicitor in London who has Uncle Frank's will. My uncle used an hotel in Bloomsbury as a base — he can check if there's anything maybe in store there."

"Good thinking," agreed Gaunt mildly and nodded at the carrier bag. "Shopping?"

"Souvenirs." Sarah Marsh flicked a smile on and off. "For our friends — might as well let them know we've really been. And the stuff's cheap."

They left him. A couple of moments later he saw them again, two straight-backed, purposeful figures in the rear seat of a jeep being driven out of the square by one of Sollas's men.

Glad to know they'd gone, he went into the Da Gama and glanced into the bar as he passed. Jaime was there, polishing tables while another youth loafed over by a window. He strongly resembled the second stone-thrower in the cemetery incident and was laughing at something Jaime had said.

"Senhor Gaunt . . . "

The clerk at the reception desk signalled him and had a letter in his hand. Taking it, Gaunt saw his name scrawled across the front in a bright blue ink and the heavy *Policia de Seguranca Publica* seal across the flap.

He went up to his room and lit a cigarette before he opened it. Sergeant Costa's broad, bold handwriting filled the single page but came down to the fact that he'd be out of Claras most of the day chasing witnesses on a robbery that had been reported. Then came the names Gaunt had wanted, five people, each with a Lisbon address, each known to have been visited by Preston the evening before he died.

Gaunt tucked the list in his wallet pocket. There were envelopes and notepaper in one of the dressing table drawers and he thought for a moment then scribbled a quick note of his own. Taking the handkerchief with the broken watch-glass, he folded it carefully, put it in an envelope with the note, sealed the envelope, then went out again.

His first stop was to leave the envelope at the policia station for Costa's return. From there, he located the village post office and had them dig out a cable form.

"Problems Here But Weather Fine." That seemed about right — he signed it, addressed it to Falconer at the Q. and L. T. R. office in Edinburgh, then let the counter clerk struggle to work out the cost.

After he'd paid, he went over to a telephone booth in the corner, checked the Lisbon directory, then dialled the British Embassy number and fed coins into the slot while the number rang out. When the embassy answered, there was the usual minute or two of delays while he battled to get past the operator and a couple of secretaries and was finally connected with the duty officer.

"Gaunt? Ah . . . " There was a pause and a noise which sounded like the embassy man sipping tea. "Yes, we had a signal about you and this Preston business. Like to come and see us about it?"

Gaunt grimaced at the receiver. That was about the last thing he had in mind. He'd learned early on in this new career that whatever the flag, embassy protocol could waste hours.

"No time," he said sadly, "I've to wrap this up quickly then get the first plane home. It's the time of year — the department pipe band practices have started."

A swallowing, spluttering sound came over the line. But duty officers were trained to keep their cool.

"I'll tell my wife," came the acid reply. "She's from Scotland too. All right, Gaunt, exactly what the hell do you want?"

"Nothing complicated," he soothed. "I'm involved with a Doctor Arthur Sollas, also a Bernard Ryan, a photographer, and a Martin Lawson, archaeologist. Can you see what you've got on them?"

"All ours?"

"As far as I know — I haven't seen their passports."

"Quite." The duty officer thawed a little. "Gaunt, have you any idea how many thousand British subjects are permanent residents in this country? How many more are just passing through? The only ones we really know about are the people who land in some kind of trouble." He paused. "Could — ah . . . "

"That's what I want to find out."

The embassy man sighed. "Well, hold on."

He'd smoked a cigarette and was thinking about another before the duty officer came back on the line.

"Doctor Sollas we know about," he said warily. "He's on the ambassador's list for cocktail receptions. Not the 'A' list, of course, but he certainly rates a 'B.' He's in private practice in Lisbon with shares in a clinic — more of a sleeping partner than anything, but he knows the right people."

"And the other two?"

"Nothing. Anything else?"

"In a way — " Gaunt hesitated — "though it's more personal . . . "

"As long as it's not money," warned the duty officer stiffly. "I've orders from the top on that — we've had too many visiting firemen wandering through and thinking we've some kind of loan office. The embassy budget can't take any more."

"Not money. Have you a *Financial Times* handy?"

"We get it air edition from London, daily. But . . . " The duty officer stopped, puzzled.

"Get it," invited Gaunt.

That took a moment or two.

"Now check a couple of prices for me, will you? Consolidated Breweries and Malters Holding Stock."

He heard a mutter of indignation then a rustle of paper.

"Consolidated closed yesterday at 124, Malters rose to 160" — a gathering interest crept into the voice at the other end — "something happening with them? I've a little money in the family piggy bank that's looking for a profitable home so — ah . . . "

Gaunt grinned. "Suppose you check

out Ryan and Lawson again, then I'll let you know."

"Yes, but . . ."

"I'll call back. Wait till then."

Gaunt hung up. When he'd bought in, Consolidated had already been shading at 130 and Maltsters had been on the upswing at 146. Now it looked as though a lot more investors were stepping into the situation. Most wouldn't stay on for the full ride, when the real risk came. They'd settle for a fast if modest profit and get out . . . while his own gamble would still just be warming up.

If it all came off, he'd had his eye on a neat little Japanese colour TV set and there could be a useful chunk of money left over. Though 'if' was a big little word.

Half an hour later he ate lunch in a café off the square. The table didn't have a cloth and the wine came in a chipped carafe, but it washed down one of the thickest steak sandwiches he'd ever seen and the bill was small enough to make him double the size of tip he'd planned.

It was warm and bright and getting

warmer when he finally drove the Fiat out to Inez Torres's bungalow. As he swung into the driveway a middle-aged woman in a green overall looked up, broke off from sweeping the front steps of the house, and went inside. By the time he'd climbed out of the car, Inez had appeared on the porch to greet him.

For a moment he said nothing, knowing he had an idiotic grin on his face but not able to do anything about it.

This was the girl he'd seen in the painting — a welcoming sparkle in her dark eyes, a smile on her lips and supple vitality in every movement. She'd chosen faded blue jeans, a gay open-necked shirt-blouse tied in front at her midriff and a matching cotton headscarf which all but hid her jet-black hair. The plain gold chain was on her wrist and she had simple, open-toed sandals.

The effect was total and complete, and he had a feeling she both knew it and enjoyed it.

"Reporting for duty, Senhor Gaunt," she said demurely. "Have you any plan for this safari?"

"No," Still looking at her, he rubbed a pensive hand along his chin. "But that's liable to change."

She laughed, a husky, pleased sound. "Well, you wanted a guide and I've thought of a few places. But remember, I have to be back in time to go to work." Her dark eyes twinkled again. "The casino management go berserk if anyone turns up late."

"But you'll be going to Estoril." He had an idea. "Look, Inez, I've people to see in Lisbon later. That means going through Estoril." He paused hopefully. "We'd have more time if I drove you there without coming back here. I could see these people, come back again to Estoril and — well, bring you home after the show."

"There's Luis — but Anna will be here." She frowned slightly, considered for a moment, then nodded. "Why not? As long as we use my car, Jonathan. The things for my act are in the trunk."

Gaunt compared the battered Fiat with the sleek lines of the Lancia and didn't feel like arguing.

"Good." Inez reached into a pocket of

her jeans and handed him the keys. "I'll tell Anna — it'll only take a moment. Then I'll say goodbye to Luis. He's round the back."

She disappeared back into the house. Putting the keys in his pocket, Gaunt strolled over to where the Lancia was parked, eyed it appreciatively then walked slowly round towards the rear of the bungalow.

Luis Torres was standing beside a rabbit hutch inside a patch of grass fenced off knee-high from the rest of the garden. He had his back to Gaunt, but turned quickly as he heard footsteps. For a moment he eyed Gaunt nervously and seemed ready to back away, then he stayed where he was, both arms round the sleek, white rabbit he was holding.

"Hello, Luis . . . *como esta?*" Gaunt kept the same unhurried pace then stopped at the fence. "Remember me?"

After a moment a slow, undecided smile crossed the thin, pale face and Torres nodded.

"Inez and I brought you home last night." Gaunt stepped over the fence, came up to him, and deliberately turned his attention to the rabbit, stroking it behind one ear. Then he looked up. "Home from the Castelo,"

"Castelo." Luis Torres got the word out with an effort then after further effort his mouth twitched again. "Senhor Gaunt."

"That's right. You like going to the Castelo, don't you?"

"Like?" The haggard face twitched and those eyes showed a struggle as if something was trapped there, trapped and fighting to get free. Suddenly Luis shook his head quickly and edged away towards the hutch, the rabbit hugged closer, looking past Gaunt towards the house.

His sister was coming. Luis brightened as she came up to him and kissed him on the cheek.

"*Adeus*, Luis." She added something quietly and Luis gave a hesitant nod.

Biting his lip he came forward slowly and held the rabbit out towards Gaunt. Gently, Gaunt let the tiny teeth nibble his fingers, saw Luis watching him anxiously, and felt a sudden, angry sympathy with what was left of Lieutenant Luis Torres.

"I'll look after her, Luis," he said quietly.

Maybe it got through, maybe it was only the tone of his voice, maybe he only imagined it. But the thin face seemed to relax, as if thanking him.

5

THE Lancia had a Zagato coachwork body, leather upholstery, a five-speed gearbox, and a high compression alloy engine which sucked fuel through twin carburettors with a muted roar.

Jonathan Gaunt treated it cautiously for the first few kilometres, watching the rev. counter and getting the feel of brakes and steering. Then, gradually, he gave the car more throttle, heard a new, tight, rasping note throb from the exhaust, and felt at home. On the next length of straight he slammed the car up through the gears and counted the seconds while the speedometer swept round.

He saw it quiver past the 170 k.p.h. mark then eased back on the accelerator as the next corner appeared ahead. Over a hundred in miles per hour in less time than his tuned Mini took to get to sixty . . . and a lot more waiting.

"Well?" Curled up comfortably in the

passenger seat, Inez Torres watched him with amusement in her eyes and an unlit cigarette held between her fingers. "Do you like her?"

"Like?" Gaunt concentrated on taking the corner then grinned as he settled back. "After this, I'll feel underprivileged."

"My agent would give you her free, gift-wrapped, if he had the chance." The cigarette lighter on the dashboard popped out and she used it. "Every time he knows I'm driving he thinks about what happened to Luis — and worries about his percentage."

"And you?" He kept his eyes on the road.

"He can go to hell." She smoked the cigarette for a moment, watching the fields and hedgerows slip past.

"Jonathan, I talked to Manuel Costa, as you asked."

Gaunt nodded, but said nothing.

"He said — well, anyway, I think I can forget about something now." She stretched lazily, like a cat, then smiled at him. "Thanks for that. Now be a good tourist and enjoy yourself. That's what I'm going to do."

First there was Sintra, a fairytale town of palaces and vast gardens of flowers high in the hills where they left the Lancia and solemnly hired a horse-drawn open garry complete with a driver who wore an old top-hat and insisted on singing.

Then the car took them north again, climbing through rocky passes and wooded gorges to Mafra, another hilltop fantasy with a castle of 5000 doors, a treasure-house library and carillon bells.

And so it went on, flickering impressions — a café in a deer park where they had coffee and tiny sweet cakes while fawns nuzzled the windows. A village without name but with a souvenir shop where Gaunt bought a featherlight white shoulder square of soft, crocheted wool when she lingered over it for a moment. And more — until at last, as they chewed candy they'd bought from a roadside vendor, the Lancia came over a rise and began murmuring down towards the blue haze of the coastline.

A few white-washed cottages became the outskirts of a fishing village with a tiny harbour and brightly painted seine-net boats which had high, sharply curved bow and stern-posts. Two kilometres on, as the road swung inland again, Inez touched Gaunt's arm and gestured towards a farm track leading off to the right.

The track, two ruts with a grassy centre strip, ended at the edge of a small, sandy bay. Off-shore, the heavy Atlantic rollers spent their white force on a reef of black rock leaving the bay a quiet, peaceful place where the water rippled in. Sea-birds were feeding along its edge and they were completely alone with not as much as another car or house in sight.

"Let's stop," said Inez almost sadly. Leaning over, her hair brushing his cheek, she switched off the engine then sat back with her eyes half-closed for a moment. "When will you go back to Britain?"

"I don't know. Maybe in a couple of days, maybe more. "Gaunt wound down his window and the steady roar of the waves breaking on the reef came flooding in.

"When you do, you can say you've

seen Cape Roca." She pointed to a broad headland of rock to the north. "*Cabo de Roca* — that's the most westerly point in Europe."

He looked at the headland, towering above the rollers pounding white around its base. It had a lighthouse and, further back, he saw a cluster of small buildings surrounded by tall, thin masts and large dish aerials.

"It looks busy," he mused. "Radar?"

"And Satellite communications. North Atlantic Treaty Organisation, maritime headquarters, Eastern Atlantic." She shrugged, her face clouding a little. "Luis was stationed there. That's when we found this beach — we used to picnic here sometimes."

He said nothing for a moment, understanding. Then, rubbing a hand along the rim of the steering wheel, he asked quietly, "What was it all about, Inez?"

She frowned. "What was what all about?"

"The panic about Luis." He waited then shrugged. "All right, I'll guess it. Last night wasn't the first time your brother slipped off after dark to the Castelo. And you were scared he might have been there the night Francis Preston died. Scared sick ever since Sergeant Costa let it slip Preston's death maybe wasn't an accident. Right?"

Inez came bolt upright, staring at him, fists knuckle-tight on her lap. Gaunt only smiled a little then lit two cigarettes and held one out towards her.

Slowly, almost reluctantly, she nodded then took the cigarette.

"Was he out that night?" asked Gaunt.

"*Sim* . . . yes, somewhere." It came like a sigh. "Anna was in the house as usual and thought he was sleeping. But I found mud on his shoes in the morning."

"And it wasn't the first time?"

"No." She looked down at her hands. "Jonathan. I know something did happen to him that night. It showed the next day — he was restless and upset, more nervous than I'd ever seen him."

"You tried asking him about it?"

"Luis?" She gave a tight, helpless smile. "Sometimes I think he does understand, sometimes I even imagine that the real

Luis is still trapped somewhere inside what he's become. Trapped and — well, trying to get out. But it just can't happen."

"Yet you say things have changed," reminded Gaunt. "Why?"

"Because I finally had the courage to ask Manuel Costa when the police thought Preston died. They say some time before midnight. Midnight?" She shook her head firmly and confidently. "Luis was still in the house at eleven-thirty, when Anna when to bed. Even if he'd run all the way, Luis couldn't have got to the Castelo in half an hour."

"So you can forget about that notion." Gaunt nodded but wondered.

"I have." She laughed, a soft, wry throb of a sound. "I should have known better." Then she noticed the dashboard clock and her eyes widened in alarm. "Jonathan, the time! I must be at that rehearsal . . . "

"You'll be there." Flicking his cigarette out of the window, Gaunt started the Lancia then, his hand resting on the gear lever, asked a last question. "Where do you think Luis did get to that night?"

"I don't know." She shook her head. "I don't suppose I'll ever know. But it doesn't matter now — and I'm going to have that window fixed so it can't happen again." Her eyes strayed to the clock again. "*Por favor* . . . please, Jonathan. If I am late . . . "

"The management will throw a fit," he completed for her. "All right, Estoril."

He slapped the car into gear.

★ ★ ★

It was near to five-thirty p.m. when they reached Estoril. A stiffening breeze from the sea had begun snapping the row of national flags outside the casino frontage and the long expanse of gardens sweeping down towards the shore road was deserted. But the casino was already preparing for the night's business. As Gaunt stopped the Lancia near the main entrance a uniformed porter hurried out to greet them and he saw cleaners working with mops and dusters on the other side of the plate-glass windows.

Sliding out, Inez had the porter take a couple of small suitcases from the boot then, as the man started back with them, she came round to Gaunt's side of the car.

"My last show is just after midnight — I can leave about one a.m.," she told him through the open window. "I'll tell them to keep a table for you. All right?"

"I'll be there." Gaunt smiled at her. "Though I may have a try at the gaming rooms first — I've a lucky feeling about today."

"That's when things usually come unstuck," she said dryly, then chuckled, "*Adeus*, Jonathan — just don't use my car as a side-bet."

She hurried after the porter. Gaunt watched till they'd disappeared into the casino, then lit a cigarette and set the Lancia moving.

It was early dusk when he made Lisbon. Stopping at a news-stand, he bought a street map of the city and spent a few minutes checking it against the list of addresses Sergeant Costa had provided, addresses which traced Francis Preston's last evening.

During the next half hour he disposed

of two, a travel agency in Avenida Aliados, in the centre of town, and a car rental firm only a couple of streets away.

At the travel agency, Preston had booked a plane seat on a London-bound flight for the following week. At the rental garage he'd paid his account up to date and had advised the desk clerk that he'd only need the car he was using for a few more days.

It was the first hint that Preston had been considering leaving. But the next address on the list took that an unexpected stage further. Doctor Arturo Burnay lived in a fashionable block of terrace houses on the fringe of old Lisbon, looking across parkland to a skyline of modern hotel blocks. A brass plate said Burnay was a consultant neurologist and when Gaunt rang the doorbell the manservant who answered treated him with the kind of smooth courtesy which added ten per cent to any medical bill.

Shown into a small, comfortably furnished study, Gaunt waited several minutes before the room door opened again. The stout, middle-aged man who entered had a round, pleasant face and thinning black hair and was in an old sports jacket and slacks.

"Doctor Burnay?" asked Gaunt, rising.

"*Sim* . . . " The man nodded cheerfully. "Forgive my dress, Senhor Gaunt. But if this is a professional visit, one usually makes an appointment . . . "

"I came because of a man named Francis Preston, Doctor," said Gaunt quietly. "The police say he was here the evening before he died."

"True." A frown creased the round face. "And your interest, senhor?"

Gaunt shrugged and twisted fact a little for simplicity's sake. "I'm working through the British Embassy, Doctor. Preston's death raises some awkward legal details we're trying to sort out."

"*Obrigado* . . . then I will help if I can." Burnay gestured him back into the chair and sat down opposite. "But you must understand that Preston did not come to me as a patient. In fact, that evening was his first visit — as well as his last."

"I'm just trying to tie up some loose

ends." Gaunt grinned a shade wearily. "As far as I can make out, he was getting ready to leave Portugal. Did you know that?"

"He told me." The neurologist offered Gaunt a cigar from a small silver box. As Gaunt shook his head, the man smiled, chose one for himself, and lit it carefully. Then, drawing on the smoke, he added, "In fact, that was what brought him here."

Gaunt frowned. "Could you explain that?"

"*Sim* . . . or I will try. Senhor Preston first telephoned for an appointment. But when he came, it was to ask me about a young man who had been under my professional care for some time."

Suddenly, Gaunt understood. "Luis Torres?"

"You know him?" Burnay lowered his cigar and looked surprised.

"Well enough to know Preston spent a lot of time with him." Gaunt sensed he was on delicate, medical ethics type ground but probed on. "Did Preston want to try to help him even more — through you?"

Burnay nodded. "He offered to pay for any medical or surgical treatment which might improve the young man's condition. But I told him the simple truth, that everything possible already had been done." His plump shoulders shrugged sadly. "Brain surgery can certainly achieve many things today which were impossible a few years ago — but not for Luis Torres. There was too much damage in that car accident."

"His sister seems to think there's still hope for improvement," murmured Gaunt.

"Is it wrong to hope?" queried Burnay quietly. "The human body can repair itself in strange ways. Even with the brain, it can confound the medical profession by unexpected recovery." He shrugged a little. "We accept it can happen, though we don't understand why. In Luis Torres's case, such a recovery would be a miracle — but even miracles can happen, and hope can sometimes help. Does hope hurt his sister?"

"I don't think it ever hurt anyone." Gaunt showed his understanding then pursed his lips for a moment and moved on. "What about Preston, Doctor? Did he hint why he was leaving Portugal?"

"No, nor did I ask." Placing the cigar carefully on a silver ashtray, Burnay rose and gave a polite but firm smile "He was a man who came and went, Senhor Gaunt. There is nothing more I can tell you."

★ ★ ★

Night had arrived outside, the sky a rich, dark velvet with stars brighter than he could ever remember having seen before. But there were still two names on the list — back behind the Lancia's wheel, Gaunt used the dashboard light and checked the street map again.

Jose Andella and Jorge Dias . . . Sergeant Costa had bracketed them in ink, then, under the addresses, had added: "Try Jeronimos Monastery first. They are on museum staff."

Gaunt knew the monastery. He'd gone there with Patti on a sightseeing tour on their honeymoon trip. He remembered a great sprawl of Manueline architecture located beside the River Tagus, its back to the city, an overwhelming grandeur of stone and stained glass.

There had been a great fountain in a broad central garden, they'd walked along tree-lined avenues — and he'd taken photographs of Patti standing beside the gigantic monument to the discoveries down at the river's edge.

It brought back other memories too. The kind he supposed he should be trying to forget — except that they still mattered. Wryly, he forced his mind back to the street map again, made sure of his route, then slipped the Lancia into gear and set off.

Lisbon's traffic was as heavy as ever, but with a difference in character. Now it was pleasure-bent. The streets seemed ribbons of neon-lit clubs and restaurants only broken by vast, flood-lit squares where more traffic swirled and hooted and swung in lane-changing aggression. The Lancia drew its share of horn-blasts and near-misses as he battled through the confusion, but at last things became quieter and the monastery appeared ahead.

Gaunt parked outside, stood for a

moment looking up at the long sweep of its stonework, then walked towards a door where he saw lights and an attendant. He gave his name and asked for Jose Andella.

"Senhor Andella?" The attendant showed an immediate respect, disappeared into a little cubicle, and used an internal telephone. After a moment he hung up, came back, and gestured Gaunt to follow him.

They walked along a series of vast stone corridors, past silent, cloistered courtyards and once he caught a distant glimpse of the discoveries monument. A choir was singing in another part of the monastery, but they went away from the sound, entered a different part of the building, and climbed a narrow stairway. At the top was a small, plain doorway. His guide knocked, waited till a muffled voice answered, then opened the door and gestured Gaunt through.

"Good evening, Senhor Gaunt." A thin, elderly man with a bald head and a neat, silvery beard rose from behind a desk in the brightly lit room. It was a long, narrow room with a high ceiling and stone walls which seemed almost lined with books.

"Senhor Andella?" queried Gaunt.

"*Sim* . . . that is correct." Andella, who wore a dark, slightly old-fashioned suit topped by a stiff white wing-collar and a large, loose bow-tie of dark red silk, nodded his thanks to the attendant. As the attendant went out and the door closed, Andella smiled a greeting. "How can I help you?"

"You're a museum official here senhor?" asked Gaunt.

"Among other things, yes." The smile remained. "My official title is executive curator of archaeology." Andella paused and considered Gaunt with a slight puzzlement. "Have you an interest in the subject?"

"Not directly," said Gaunt. "More in a visitor you had a few nights ago, an Englishman."

"Francis Preston?" Andella refused to show surprise. "I see. Is this interest — ah — personal, Senhor Gaunt?"

"I work for a British government department," said Gaunt carefully. "That gives me no particular official status — but

173

you can check with our embassy. Or this might do." He produced his Remembrancer's Department warrant card.

"Por favor . . . ?" Andella took the card, studied it for a moment, then gave a dry chuckle and handed it back. "I have an idea now why you are here, Senhor Gaunt. Francis Preston told me a strange story about a disagreement he had with your department over some church plate you classed as Treasure Trove. Now he is dead, you are anxious to find where that church plate might be, eh?"

"That's how it started," agreed Gaunt neutrally. "Now I've got other problems."

"I see." Andella looked at him oddly then turned, dumped some books from a chair to the floor, and brought the chair nearer his desk. "I don't know where your Treasure Trove is hidden, Senhor Gaunt. But sit down — tell me of these 'other problems'."

Gaunt took the chair and waited till the other man was again behind his desk. Andella had keen, bright eyes, sharp enough to make him wonder how far he could go.

"The police say Preston came to see you the evening before he died," Gaunt began slowly.

"In this room," nodded Andella. "A colleague and I discussed certain matters with him."

"Was the colleague's name Jorge Dias?"

"*Sim* . . . you are well informed." Andella tugged his beard a little and frowned. "Let me save you some time, Senhor Gaunt. Jorge Dias left Lisbon today for Italy, to give a series of lectures to students in Rome. He — ah — is our expert in a certain field of archaeology."

"Meaning early Roman remains in Portugal?" asked Gaunt bluntly.

Andella winced then spread his hands apologetically. "Very well informed, I should have said . . . forgive an old man's childishness. So you know about Claras?"

"Arthur Sollas showed me round this morning," Gaunt smiled at the museum executive's discomfiture. "He also told me Preston hoped to find something a whole lot bigger than that villa. But he didn't seem to know Preston was planning to leave Portugal — did you?"

Andella nodded slowly. "Preston came to tell us — and to see if there was no way in which the Claras excavations might have erred." He toyed absently with a pen which had been lying on the desk then shook his head, a trace of amusement in his voice. "Though the man is dead, Senhor Gaunt, I must confess Dias and I rather enjoyed the situation. Especially as we had to tell him there was no error. After all, we never did suggest anything more than the villa was there."

It was Gaunt's turn to be puzzled. He leaned forward, frowning. "You mean you knew it was there? I thought . . . "

"You thought Francis Preston had produced another piece of brilliant deductive discovery?" Andella sniffed and chuckled. "You don't know much about archaeology, Senhor Gaunt."

"No," admitted Gaunt grimly. "But I'm willing to learn."

"*Obrigado,*" declared the older man acidly. "Then the first thing to understand is this man Preston — whom I still liked. Preston the amateur who went round the world rubbing professional noses in the dirt with his discoveries?" He made a noise surprisingly close to a raspberry. "That part was a fake, a clever public relations creation."

"I could call that professional jealousy," mused Gaunt.

Andella flushed almost angrily. "Senhor Gaunt, I can name you distinguished colleagues in half a dozen countries who will say the same. Archaeology is cursed by hair-brained idiots who use everything from bulldozers to tame clairvoyants in their search for fame. Preston's only difference was that he was much more clever. When he started a project he was already half-sure of success — because of other men's work!"

"You mean someone else found that villa before him?"

"Yes, almost fifty years ago — some students from Lisbon on a summer school camp. They positively established that they were dealing with the site of a second century B.C. villa, and it has been on our records ever since. But of course, all they did was nibble at the location."

Coming from behind the desk, Andella walked over to the window at the far end of the room, looked out at the city's night skyline for a moment, then turned. His voice had a bitter edge.

"We have a rich past, Senhor Gaunt. But today you could call us poor but proud — perhaps too proud. We are full partners in NATO. We cling to a scatter of colonies, mostly by sheer military presence. But do you know the cost? We spend more of our earnings on defence than any other country in Western Europe. There is little money left over for luxuries."

"And none for digging up Roman villas?"

"Let us say the Claras villa stayed far down the list of our priorities." The museum man grimaced. "So when a private syndicate suggested they would meet the cost we were interested. When they agreed that all finds would belong to our national museums — well, would you have said no to a man with money like Georges Salvador?"

"Salvador?" The unexpected name made Gaunt sit up. "I thought he was just their landlord . . . "

Andella seemed to smile into his silvery beard. "I can assure you, Senhor Gaunt, that whatever you may have heard the first interest in the Claras site came from Georges Salvador. Then he in turn interested Senhor Preston — who, of course, as an archaeologist of some popular fame carried out all the formal negotiations with the authorities."

"No inspired hunches?" Gaunt scrubbed his long jaw wryly. "All right, if Salvador is a sleeping partner in the dig what's his particular angle?"

"Angle?" Andella frowned, then understood. "Ah — unofficially, a certain tourist hotel development is planned for Claras. It is a pleasant spot, but shall we say that an historic Roman villa, newly uncovered, might be a very useful attraction?"

"Very useful, if you were an investor." Gaunt could imagine the kind of selling job Georges Salvador had carried out in interesting Francis Preston — and for once it looked as if Preston had been hoodwinked in the process. "But it wouldn't exactly please Preston when he found out."

"If he found out," qualified Andella uneasily. "When he came here that last evening he was hardly happy. But all he talked about was his personal disappointment concerning the site — and financial rumours are no concern of this department, Senhor Gaunt." He built a sad, contemplative steeple with his fingertips. "We could only tell him what facts we knew about the Claras villa, facts we could have told him at any time if he had taken the trouble to ask. We even showed him a plan drawing of what we had expected him to find."

"Could I see it?"

"*Sim.*" Andella opened a filing cabinet, carefully selected a folder, and spread out a folded sheet on a small table as Gaunt came over. "This was based on the original student dig — and our experience of similar villas in other areas."

One glance showed Gaunt that the drawing was close enough in basic detail to the plan he'd been shown by Arthur Sollas. There were only minor variations and a few extended dotted lines.

"What about these?" he asked.

"Water supply and drainage," shrugged Andella. "The Romans were highly civilised people."

"I'd heard," agreed Gaunt. He studied the drawing again then nodded his thanks. "Did Preston seem to know he'd been fooled?"

"A man like Francis Preston would not admit such a thing," murmured Andella, folding the sheet and putting it away. He closed the filing cabinet drawer then faced Gaunt again. "Now, *por favor* . . . can I ask why all this interests you so much, Senhor Gaunt?"

"Why do you think, Senhor Andella?" countered Gaunt neutrally.

Jose Andella looked at him for a long moment then very slowly shook his head.

"I would prefer to wait," he said softly. "But if you need any further help, you have only to ask."

★ ★ ★

Gaunt ate in a little café near the waterfront where the tables were crowded and the view was out towards the Salazar Bridge — a high, moving ribbon of headlights in the night as heavy traffic crossed the Tagus in both directions.

A young, surprisingly pretty girl, one of several at the bar, watched him for a spell. She finally came over to Gaunt's table as he finished a plate of *Cozido* . . . a mixture of boiled beef, ham and smoked sausage with various unidentifiable vegetables stirred in. She wore the inevitable low-cut blouse and short skirt, the blond wig clashed with natural black eyebrows, and her smile was as old an introduction as time itself.

Gaunt's answer was a fractional headshake. Shrugging, unperturbed, she wandered back to her perch at the bar and resumed her scrutiny of the tables.

Finishing his meal, he paid the bill then squeezed his way through to a telephone booth near the doors. Inside, it smelled of garlic and cheap cigars as he dialled the British Embassy number.

The duty officer he'd spoken to that morning wasn't available but the voice who answered reacted to his name.

"Gaunt? I've a message for you," came the cheerful greeting. "I've to say we're still trying and you should contact us in the morning. Oh — and I've to say thanks for something or other — he said you'd understand."

Gaunt hung up, hoping that didn't mean what he thought it might. But impetuous duty officers sometimes had to learn the hard way. Finding more change, he lifted the receiver again.

This time, his call was to the police station at Claras. Sergeant Costa's normally lazy voice briskened when he heard who was calling.

"Where are you?" demanded Costa.

"Lisbon — but I'm heading for Estoril." Gaunt lit a cigarette one-handed as a defence against the booth's atmosphere. "You got my note?"

"*Sim* . . . this afternoon, when I got back to Claras." Costa's voice dropped a conspiratorial tone or two. "You guessed right about the watch-glass. Pereira's wrist-watch is being repaired at a jeweller's shop here — he said it had been damaged at work."

183

"Anything more on him?" asked Gaunt grimly.

"Not yet — nothing on record at headquarters, at any rate." Costa paused, then chuckled. "I told them he might be involved in those burglaries we have had lately. Has — ah — Lisbon been interesting?"

"I'll tell you when I get back," answered Gaunt. "But don't wait up for me."

"I won't." Costa sighed over the line. "Can one ask why you are going to Estoril, my friend?"

"One can ask," admitted Gaunt solemnly. "But one needn't expect an answer."

He hung up, grinning, and went out to the car.

★ ★ ★

Even allowing for inevitable professional cool towards a persistently lucky amateur, the new view he'd been offered of Francis Preston shattered some previous notions and if anything left the whole tangled puzzle more complex than before. Preston had come to Portugal believing he had a chance of achieving new, almost guaranteed success at minimum cost. Except it hadn't happened — and either he'd kept his feelings tightly bottled to protect a painfully built reputation or those people who had experienced his wrath were maintaining a very deliberate silence.

He considered the second prospect for a moment, a frown crossing his freckled face. Once or twice Arthur Sollas had shown a trace of embarrassment. How much had he known in advance — how much did he know of it all even now? In the beginning it had been Georges Salvador, who had spun some kind of a story to Preston — but how did the chain go from there?

And after Preston had visited the Jeronimos Monastery that night, after he'd been told the full truth about the long-held knowledge of the villa's existence?

The easy guess was that he'd driven back to Claras in a black anger. But Francis Preston was a more complicated individual than most. Perhaps he'd still refused to accept what he'd been told because he'd already convinced himself otherwise.

Stubborn pride could have taken him to the Castelo de Rosa that night, to look again, to think, to try to force some new inspiration which might yet bring success . . .

A loud horn-blast and a flashing of headlights from the rear jerked Gaunt's attention back to his driving. Easing nearer the kerb, he grinned as a small open M.G. sports car snarled past, the lone driver waving a hand in thanks. Another few moments and the M.G. was far ahead, a pair of red tail lights which disappeared round a corner.

He'd lost the thread. If there was a thread to lose — giving up, Gaunt switched off the radio, fed the Lancia more accelerator, and drew pleasure from the way the engine note quickened.

Two kilometres on, he saw the M.G. again, stopped at a filling station. A few minutes more and the lights of Estoril were ahead. He turned off the main road at the casino, purred the Lancia up towards the car park area at the rear, and reversed into a gap in one of the rows of vehicles.

Switching off engine and lights, Gaunt climbed out. The car park was a pool of dark shadows but he could hear music and laughter coming from the casino's windows. Locking the car, he started walking towards the main entrance.

Halfway there, he slowed a little with a growing feeling he wasn't alone, an odd uneasiness which seemed concentrated between his shoulder-blades.

"Senhor Gaunt?"

The voice was soft and came from one of the darker patches of shadow beside a large Mercedes. He peered, saw a figure waiting in the shadow, and stopped.

"*Senhor . . .* " the figure took a slow step forward, still half-hidden.

At the same time, a faint rustle of movement reached Gaunt's ears, from behind. He spun instinctively — and a blow from a short, heavy rubber truncheon, aimed at his head, brushed his shoulder instead. The man who'd crept up on him snarled, cursed, and raised his arm for a second blow.

Retreating, Gaunt stopped with his

back against the radiator of another car and a new threat materialising, a third man who had appeared on his other side and was coming in at a rush with a knife.

Hands pressing for support against the cold metal behind him, Gaunt swung his right leg in a fast, vicious upward arc. He felt the jar as his heel took the knife-man low in the stomach, heard breath explode from the figure's pain-twisted mouth, and saw him stagger back, folding and almost falling.

Tight-lipped, Gaunt retreated again. But the man with the cosh was still on his left and the original figure who had hailed him was closing in from the right. They came unhurriedly, accepting they'd lost the initial surprise but professionals who had done it all before — professionals who knew as many attack variations as a football forward line and needed fewer signals.

He could shout for help. But even if he was heard above the music and noise of the casino any kind of help from there would come too late. He had seconds left, seconds while these two tormented him by waiting for their comrade with the knife to draw breath and join the finale.

Yet Gaunt felt very calm. Calm enough to register that all three men wore black sweaters and slacks with soft plimsols and to notice that the man who had hailed him, his face a wolfish blur in the dim light, also had one of those stubby little truncheons.

Suddenly, it was like being back on one of those army night combat courses where a paratroop sergeant had first taught him to hate — hate sergeants, at any rate. You let the trained, conditioned part of your mind take over while the rest remained detached because it was really happening to someone else.

"Do unto others before they do it to you . . . " The old chorus from a bawdy barrack-room song swept into his thoughts. And simultaneously Gaunt catapulted out at the weakest link, which was still the man with the knife.

Taken off guard, the man sliced a wild, upward arc with the blade left elbow slamming knife arm wide, Gaunt slid under its threat. His right hand grabbed that black sweater near the throat, his whole body impetus went behind a slamming head-butt which took his opponent full-face.

It brought a bubbling scream, half-smothered behind smashed lips and crushed nasal cartilage.

Side-stepping clear, Gaunt still wasn't quick enough to avoid the others. A truncheon took him near the collarbone with close to paralysing force, he swayed as much as dodged the other truncheon, and missed as he tried a retaliatory judo hand-stab at the nearest throat.

For a moment, footwork got Gaunt clear. But he collided with the side of a car, stumbled, recovered, warded off another blow — then the two remaining men forced him back against the vehicle. Pinned there, he braced himself as one of the truncheons swept up again.

But it stopped, still poised over his head, the whole scene bathed in a sudden, blinding glare of lights. Tyres screamed and an engine bellowed while the same lights rushed towards them.

It was the little M.G. It stopped by the simple process of slamming into the car where Gaunt was held, the driver coming out as if propelled by an ejector seat, an old-fashioned starting handle swinging in one hand.

Abandoning him, Gaunt's attackers faced this new arrival with a momentary uncertainty. Then the nearest snarled, sprang forward — and howled in agony as the starting handle blurred round to smash against his forearm with bone-breaking force.

Fear in his eyes, the truncheon falling from his limp, useless hand, the thug quickly backed away. Snuffling with pain, the injured knifeman was already staggering off into the night.

But Gaunt froze where he was, and suddenly the M.G. driver did the same. The third man was also beginning to edge back, but he was going slowly, and the automatic pistol which had appeared in his right fist stayed pointed in a threat that didn't need words.

The figures continued to fade back. A few more yards, then even the gun owner abandoned any pretence and began running. Another moment and the night had swallowed him up.

The only sound in the car park was the M.G. driver's sigh of disappointment as he lowered the starting handle.

"Thanks," said Gaunt shakily, moistening his lips. "That was getting nasty. *Muito obrigado . . .* "

"Leave it at thanks, friend." His rescuer, chunky and fair-haired, spoke with an unmistakably American accent and grinned. "Hell, it takes me all my time to ask for the men's room in Portuguese. You're British?"

"Yes." Gaunt tried to rub life back into his shoulder, still numbed from the truncheon blow. "Well, they say the U.S. cavalry always arrive on cue."

"Make it Navy," corrected the other man, tossing the starting handle into the back of the M.G. "The name's Tom Harris." He paused and inspected Gaunt carefully. "Are you all right?"

"There's nothing a drink wouldn't cure. And I owe you one while I'm at it." Gaunt held out his hand. "I'm Jonathan Gaunt. Navy or army, your timing was good."

"It's a gift," said Harris modestly. He wore a sports jacket with a plaid shirt and string tie and had a bear-crushing grip. Turning, he considered the front of his car. "A couple of fresh dents, but they'll hammer out again. Well, do we whistle up the *policia* or — ah — was it private?"

"Just a plain, old-fashioned mugging," said Gaunt with more conviction than he felt. "But they'll be far away by now — and I don't think they'll be back. Suppose we tidy up here then find that drink?"

"A reasonable attitude." Harris nodded solemn agreement.

He climbed into the M.G., fired the engine, and sent it in a screaming reverse which ended with the little car tucked away in a space at the far end of the row.

The front of the other car was going to need a new grille. Gaunt peeled off some escudo notes, tucked them under one of the wiper blades, then saw the abandoned truncheon lying on the ground. He picked it up, felt the weight of lead inside the black rubber, and tucked it carefully in a trouser pocket as Harris walked back.

He'd called what had happened a plain, old-fashioned mugging. But these men had known his name, which meant they must have been watching for the Lancia coming to the casino. And any sensible professional would have stuck that gun in his ribs as an introduction, not kept it as a last-gasp deterrent.

Unless somebody, somewhere, both knew a lot about his movements — and considered him enough of an annoyance to be put out of action though not important enough to be killed.

Dead civil servants could be an embarrassment. It was a useful consolation.

6

GAUNT'S first whisky went down with only a suspicion of contact with his throat. He ordered another and a refill of bourbon for Tom Harris, then hooked his legs more comfortably round the chrome-framed stool in the casino's lobby bar.

"Better now?" queried Harris mildly.

"A lot better." Gaunt found his cigarettes, lit one, and offered the pack to Harris as an afterthought.

"Never use them, thanks." Harris signalled the bartender. "Any peanuts left?"

"*Sim*, Lieutenant." The bartender nodded cheerfully and slid a bowl along the counter. "Extra salted, the way you like."

"They seem to know you," said Gaunt, watching Harris munch a handful. "Does that make you a regular customer, Lieutenant?"

"In a moderate way." Harris grinned

good-humouredly. "Once-a-week Mad-money Harris, that's me. A few of us from Disneyland make a weekly date to pool a few dollars against the tables. The old law of averages says we've got to win sometime."

"Disneyland?" Gaunt was as puzzled as he looked. "Like to translate that one?"

"Office of the C.-in-C. NATO, Eastern Atlantic." Harris raised his glass in a mock toast then took a swallow. "Ask any cab driver — we're located just this side of Lisbon, beside the main road. Flagpoles and concrete shoe box architecture gone mad, but that's where it all happens."

Gaunt raised an eyebrow. "I thought Cape Roca . . . " he began.

"Cape Roca is Super Disneyland," said Harris succinctly. "That's where the electronic hardware is located. Read all about it in any tourist handbook." He grinned at Gaunt. "Sir, are you by any chance an agent of some unfriendly power?"

"Yes, but I'm off duty," confided Gaunt solemnly.

"Good. I'd hate like hell to have to tell Security." Harris chuckled to himself. "They're busy anyway. Somebody lost the admiral's laundry last weekend and that's got top priority." He helped himself to another handful of peanuts, chewed, and then admitted, "Still, it isn't so bad. Mostly full speed ahead and damn the martinis and I've had my share of the other kind. Uh — you were driving that Lancia I passed on the road, weren't you?"

Gaunt nodded.

"Nice car, very nice. So if I hadn't stopped at that filling station . . . " Harris stopped and became suddenly serious. "You're sure it was a mugging?"

"What else?" queried Gaunt calmly.

"Then these Portuguese have an odd way of doing things. We've some characters back home who could give them lessons." Frowning a little, Harris rubbed his chin. Then he glanced at his watch and gave a whistle of surprise. "Hey, I'm going to be late!"

"Mad-money time?"

"Uh-huh." Harris finished his drink at a gulp. "Blackjack tonight, and I've got the kitty in my hip pocket. The boys will cut my throat if I don't show up." He realised what he'd said and grinned as he slipped down from the stool. "Figure of speech. Anyway, nice meeting you, and watch your back next time, friend." He was on his way out of the bar before Gaunt could reply.

With another hour to kill before Inez's midnight floor show appearance, Gaunt took his time about finishing his drink. Then he decided against another and went exploring.

The main lobby of Estoril's casino looked more like a brightly-lit shopping arcade than a through route to serious gambling. A broad sweep of polished marble floor was punctuated by ornamental fountains, leather couches and strategically placed greenery, the whole area edged by expensive little boutiques offering everything from Paris perfume to airline tickets.

He homed on the steady, mechanical whirring of fruit machines. Several close-packed rows of them were located in a partitioned area outside the main gambling salon, a tactful separation of pin-money addicts from the real action, and the custom seemed a mixture of goggle-eyed package tourists and local layabouts. Most of the one-armed bandits were being worked as fast as they could be fed and he watched cynically for a few minutes, seeing the tourist plug on determinedly while the locals stuck to the wiser policy of settling for a small win, priming the machine one turn on, then cashing in.

The main salon was very different. He had to show his passport to enter a vast, almost reverently hushed cathedral of a room lit by candelabra, the rows of tables quietly busy and offering everything from roulette and boule to punto banco and blackjack. Most of the clientele were in evening dress, women glittering with jewellery and their hair stiffly lacquered, their escorts grimly devoid of expression.

Tom Harris was over a blackjack table, surrounded by a group of similarly muscular, purposeful gamblers. Looking up, he saw Gaunt and waved a greeting then returned to the fray.

Five hundred escudos bought Gaunt a handful of chips and he eased along to the nearest roulette table, content to stick with the old, safe-stake play of pair and rouge, six-block and singleton.

A blonde in peach silk with an unbelievable bust was the only player to avoid the croupier's rake on the first couple of spins of the wheel. It was a clean sweep third time, and he felt lucky to win a few chips back on the six-block the next time round.

"I warned you," murmured a sardonic voice close to his ear. "Sometimes a man can spread his luck too thinly."

He turned. Immaculate in black tie and dinner jacket, Georges Salvador stood behind him, a thin smile of greeting on his lips. But it stopped there and the man's eyes examined Gaunt with a cold, almost clinical curiosity.

"The way I'm playing is meant to be a scientific approach," said Gaunt wryly. He glanced at the table and grimaced. "Something's gone wrong with the recipe, that's all. What's your method?"

"One that needs money." Deliberately, Salvador used a one thousand escudo plaque to scratch along his small moustache. "Given money, luck is self-generating."

"Old Portuguese proverb?" queried Gaunt.

"Experience, Senhor Gaunt." Salvador repeated the thin smile while the wheel began spinning again. "How has the rest of your day gone?"

"Patchy is the best word — patchy but interesting." Gaunt paused and deliberately lit a cigarette before he went on. "For instance, I looked in at the Jeronimos Monastery. They've got quite a museum there."

A strange flicker crossed Salvador's face, but he nodded. "You like museums, Senhor Gaunt?"

"I liked this one," parried Gaunt. "I learned a few things — and not just about the exhibits. You're a" — he grinned a little — "well, let's say a modest man, Senhor Salvador. When do you plan to start building that tourist hotel at Claras?"

Salvador's expression stayed frozen for a moment then he shrugged and gave a noise which might have been a laugh.

"Soon. It depends on some financial details."

"With Arthur Sollas among the shareholders?"

"Doctor Sollas?" Salvador's attitude seemed to thaw again in a way that left Gaunt puzzled. "The — ah — arrangement you seem to know about was between myself and Preston. Sollas is happy enough with his Roman villa and later" — he gave another shrug, his voice sinking to a confidential murmur — "well, if he should find out a little of the truth will it really matter? But I would think it — ah — unfortunate, even cruel to take away the sense of achievement he enjoys at the moment."

"Meaning you're telling me to keep my mouth shut?" asked Gaunt tonelessly.

"*Por favor* . . . "a wince of distaste crossed the plump sallow face. "I would phrase it more delicately. There are more than business considerations involved. Francis Preston, for instance — a dead man's personal reputation might be at stake."

"How about your own?" asked Gaunt bluntly.

Salvador shrugged and looked past him as a sudden murmur rose from the roulette table. The blonde in peach silk was very deliberately pushing every chip she possessed towards the rouge slot on the table. The wheel spun, the ball bounced round — and it settled on black. As the croupier's rake swept in, the blonde rose tight-lipped and walked away.

"Some people have to gamble for the luxuries in life," said Salvador softly. "Others . . . " he paused, suddenly hard-eyed. "A wise man might prefer the offer of a business arrangement, free from risk and suitably rewarding. Particularly if the matter involved did not really concern him."

"He might," mused Gaunt, his freckled face staying mild. "But how about if he told you to go to hell?"

Salvador gave a cynical grimace of disbelief. "Then I would give him a second chance and tell him to think again. I might even warn him not to meddle in matters beyond his own little world of form-filling government departments." He stopped and switched to a sudden smile. "A second chance, Senhor Gaunt. And my arrangements are always generous. Think about it."

Without waiting for an answer, he went away. As the dinner-jacketed figure vanished among the gambling tables, Gaunt shrugged and considered the few chips left in his hand. He got them down on the roulette table in a last spread just ahead of the croupier spinning the wheel, was conscious of the ball starting its clattering ride, then ignored it, wondering if Arthur Sollas could really have committed himself to the Claras dig on the mere strength of Preston's invitation.

And if he had, how he'd react to the news that he'd been manipulated . . .

The croupier coughed politely and the rake made a gentle tapping sound on the table. Surprised, Gaunt looked down at the twin stacks of chips which had been pushed his way. It seemed he'd won.

But only on one spin. Soberly, he collected his winnings, tossed a couple of chips back towards the table-man, and eased away to cash the rest. He had his own personal gamble under way now, without being completely sure of the stakes — except that they seemed to be growing by the moment.

★ ★ ★

It was a few minutes short of midnight when Gaunt went into the casino's night-club. It was busy and getting busier by the moment, but when he gave his name a waiter led him to a small table near the back then vanished and returned with a glass of whisky and a carafe of water.

"*Quanto* . . . how much?" asked Gaunt, reaching for his pocket.

The man shock his head. "On the house, senhor. I will tell Maria-Inez you are here, okay?"

Gaunt thanked him, tasted the whisky, then settled back and looked around. It was a plush setting with a mainly tourist audience and the show on stage was tailored to match, a line-up of topless go-go girls backed by a band earning its keep with amplified enthusiasm.

A couple of skinny males in black joined the line-up for a final frenetic routine before the dancers high-kicked off to a scatter of indifferent applause. The band sat back, there was a pause while the lighting dimmed and the whole room gradually changed in mood, then suddenly a single white spot-light pinned on the centre of the stage. A loud, demanding chord came from an unseen guitar and as the conversation in the smoke-filled room stilled a small, confident figure in a long, simply cut dress of black silk appeared in the spot-light's glare.

Inez Torres quietly adjusted the traditional black lace *fadista* shawl around her shoulders, smiling a little, seeming to absorb something of the throbbing rhythm from the guitar, but still letting her audience settle. At last, she gave a nod, the guitar's throb sank to background level, and she began.

Fado meant fate, *fadista* songs all spoke of human needs and frailties — and that motionless figure in black sang of love and sadness in a voice of elemental, demanding clarity which held and trapped and stirred.

The words didn't have to be understood, hardly mattered. The room seemed to hold only that timeless voice and the simplicity of the guitar. Before the first song ended a woman at the next table to Gaunt had tears running down her cheeks. When the song did finish there was a silence for a moment which was as much of a tribute as the storm of applause that followed.

The guitar began again, Inez shifted her stance just a little . . .

In all, she sang four *fado* songs, each stripping its way down through her audience's emotions. Then, suddenly, it was over. The lights came back on, the magic ended, a dazed roomful of people finished their applause, and as the figure in black left a knock-about juggling act took over. It was largely ignored. The casino audience had experienced something from which it took time to recover and adjust.

When the juggling act ended the go-go girls stormed back on again. Gaunt had ordered another drink when he saw Inez come towards him from a side door he hadn't noticed before. She was wearing a lime green dress with a scooped neckline, her black hair was caught up high on her head, and the transformation let her move between the tables without being recognised.

Reaching him, she sat down, took the cigarette he offered, and cupped one hand round his lighter so that their fingers touched lightly. Then, after a long draw on the cigarette, she sat back with a sigh.

"Tired?" he asked.

"Recovering." She grimaced a little. "With *fado*, switching off afterwards is the problem."

The drink he'd ordered arrived but she didn't want anything and sat smoking the cigarette, absently watching the floor show. Suddenly, she brightened.

"I telephoned home before the first performance. Anna says everything's fine — Luis was sleeping."

"Good." Gaunt nodded vaguely, his thoughts for the moment back on the chances of any more trouble happening at the car park.

"Jonathan?" She hesitated, puzzled at his mood. "What's wrong?"

"Nothing that matters." He shook his head reassuringly but saw no harm in telling her part of it. "Inez, I saw a Doctor Burnay in Lisbon."

She frowned. "I know him."

"Preston went to him to ask if there was any way he could help Luis. Preston would have footed the bill."

"I didn't know — but he was like that." Inez smiled a little, but sadly. "He spent a lot of time with Luis. Sometimes, he'd bring books or games, like I told you — he was a good man."

Who would still go along with a vaguely crooked proposition when it suited his own ends. Gaunt looked over at the twisting go-go girls for a moment and grinned at the thought.

"They're from England," said Inez maliciously and chuckled, drawing her own conclusions. "You'd be disappointed. They're all tweeds and pearls back-stage."

He gave her a mock scowl of protest. "Why shatter the illusion? I was enjoying it."

"Then if we stay here I'll tell you the rest," she countered with amusement. "Like how two of them are married with children and . . . " she laughed and stopped at his expression. "On the other hand, you could take me home. This is where I work, remember?"

"Fine." Gaunt had had enough of smoke and the amplified noise. He pushed back his chair then stopped. "Anything to collect back-stage?"

"A coat, that's all."

He nodded, glad of the excuse. "Then I'll bring the car round front while you get it."

She looked mildly surprised but agreed.

★ ★ ★

Outside, there was still the same darkly clouded night with occasional, filtered moonlight. But the car park was empty of life and Gaunt relaxed his grip on the rubber truncheon in his pocket then climbed aboard the Lancia.

Inez was waiting at the casino main door, a light coat draped over her shoulders. Once she was in the passenger seat, he set the car moving and turned north on the coast road, keeping a careful eye on the rear view mirror.

They weren't followed. Satisfied as

much as relieved, Gaunt settled back and glanced briefly at the girl by his side. Her face was a finely sculptured silhouette in the dim light from the facia instruments and that light, tantalising perfume she used teased at his senses.

Forty-eight hours before he hadn't known she existed. Yet now, she was one person Gaunt felt he knew enough about to trust — and something more, something rooted deeper that scarred instincts told him to avoid admitting. Because when he did, Patti was somehow there in the background. And Patti had another man now, another man whose name and bed she shared as if Gaunt had never existed.

But whether that part was self-pity or something worse, he didn't want to try to work out. It had happened, it was over.

Inez had the radio switched on low to a music station and was lying back on the seat, humming under her breath as the car purred along.

"Do you know what I'd like to do?" she asked suddenly.

"No. But I'll listen." He grinned sideways at her.

"Kick off my shoes and walk on sand."
She gave a small, almost apologetic laugh.
"That's stupid, isn't it?"

He shook his head and kept his eyes
on the road, deliberately.

"I can think of a place," he told her.
"I even think I could find the way."

"*Por favor* . . . let's try." She made a
small, contented noise in her throat. Her
long, slim legs stretched cat-like in front
of her as she shifted in her seat, then her
hair brushed his cheek. "Jonathan, who
was she — this girl who stays in your
mind?" Solemn eyes considered him for
a moment, "Don't look so surprised. Any
woman knows the signs."

"My wife — ex-wife now." Gaunt
answered more curtly than he meant.
Talking about it hurt too. "She — well,
things didn't work out."

"That's what I thought." Inez smiled to
herself then added quietly: "I'm someone
else, Jonathan. All I ask is you remember
that."

She came closer against him while
the car purred on, headlights forming
a bright corridor through the night.

At the little bay near Cape Roca he

stopped the Lancia near the fringe of the beach. As the engine died, they were left with the steady crash of waves on the shore and the piping calls of seabirds feeding just above the surf-line. In the distance, the clustered lights on the Cape and what they stood for had a twinkling unreality as if another world away.

They left the car and walked a little way, hand in hand, not talking, the sea and the busy, piping cries a constant, soothing background. At last they stopped and Gaunt very gently brought her nearer till the warmth of her body was against his own.

When he kissed her, she seemed to shiver a little then it passed and her lips were searching too, her whole body meeting and answering his hunger.

It seemed a long time afterwards when they returned to the car. They shared a cigarette there, Inez's head on his shoulder. Finally, Gaunt eased round, flicked the glowing stub that remained out into the night, then faced her again and kissed her.

"Inez . . ."

"No." She shook her head and put a

serious finger against his lips. "Don't say anything, Jonathan. Not now — please."

She waited till he nodded, then smiled. "Now take me home before Anna gets worried and starts thinking about telephoning Manuel Costa."

"And Sergeant Costa wouldn't be amused?" Gaunt sighed, started the engine, and let it idle for a second. Then, reluctantly, he slipped the Lancia into gear and set it jolting over the rough track, away from the shore and back to the road.

They reached Claras at two a.m., passed through its sleeping square while a clock tower chimed, and soon were driving up the narrow lane which led to Inez's bungalow.

But as the Lancia reached the end of the lane and the house showed ahead, Gaunt found the kind of surprise waiting he could have done without. The bungalow was a blaze of light, three police cars were lying outside it, and armed, uniformed men seemed everywhere around.

He heard a gasp from Inez, then she gripped his arm. Gaunt slowed the car to a crawl and brought it to a halt beside the other vehicles. Two policemen with leather jackets and shoulder-slung machine-pistols met them as they climbed out, but another figure darted from the bungalow and shoved forward. Sergeant Manuel Costa's habitually lazy attitude had vanished, and his thin, sallow face was hard and grim.

"Inez." His greeting was a curt nod which ignored Gaunt. "I have been trying to contact you."

"Why?" Apprehension in her voice, she looked past him towards the house. "Has — has something happened to Luis?"

"We want him." Costa thumbed back towards the house. "Your housekeeper said he was in his room. But he isn't there now."

She moistened her lips. "Manuel . . . "

"For tonight I am Sergeant Costa," corrected the detective with a moment's gentleness. "*Desculpe-me* . . . truly, I'm sorry. But this is no social call."

"What's happened then?" asked Gaunt, taking a casual step forward. He stopped short and blinked as one of the policemen prodded a machine-pistol muzzle firmly into his stomach. "And tell him to be careful with that damned thing — it might go off!"

Costa knocked the gun away with a scowl and followed it up with a snarled order which sent the uniformed men fading back.

"Well?" asked Gaunt patiently.

For a moment Costa didn't answer, his hands rammed deep into the pockets of the light raincoat he was wearing, his face a stony, unhappy mask swept by the glow from the police cars' whirring turret lamps. Then he shrugged.

"An hour ago, one of our patrol cars found an abandoned vehicle. Or they thought it was abandoned, till they looked inside — there were two people dead inside."

"Who, Manuel?" It came from Inez like a whisper of fear.

"Senhor Preston's nephew and his wife." Costa met Gaunt's fractionally lifted eyebrow and nodded. "Murdered — stabbed and viciously beaten to death. Almost certainly both died away from the car. But they were dragged back to it afterwards, then an attempt was made to set it on fire."

"And you think that Luis . . . " Inez stared at him as if hypnotised then flared defensively. "You are supposed to be his friend! Or would you rather forget that?"

Costa winced and shook his head. "The car was on a side-road only a few kilometres from here." He brought a hand from one pocket, the fingers holding something already tagged inside a small plastic bag. "We found this beside it, Inez."

It was a battered, ordinary, gun-metal cigarette lighter. But one glance brought a sound like a moan from the girl at Gaunt's side.

"You recognise it?" asked Costa quietly.

She nodded, unable to speak.

"So did I." Bitterly, Costa brought out his other hand to show Gaunt a twin of the lighter. "Luis and I bought these together, years ago, in the same *tabaco* store. We spent an extra three escudos we could ill afford to have our initials engraved on them." He held the lighters closer, the worn lettering still plain. "See for yourself — 'M.C.' for Manuel Costa, 'L.T.' for Luis Torres." He shrugged. "Luis does not smoke now. But I have seen him still carrying this lighter. You agree, Inez?"

"He does," she confirmed in a low, weary voice. "He — he keeps it like a toy."

"Perhaps now you understand, Senhor Gaunt?" asked Costa tonelessly.

"You've got his lighter," said Gaunt stubbornly. "But you're still talking about a man who'd be more likely to run and hide if he saw a stranger. What the hell would he want to kill anyone for?"

"Can I answer that before we find him?" Costa shook his head helplessly. "I would like that to be soon. For the moment, I am still in charge here. But headquarters are sending men and when that happens . . . " He left it unfinished.

"All I know is that Anna said he was in the house when I telephoned, Manuel," said Inez. She looked around at the night and bit her lip. "Perhaps he heard your cars, perhaps he was frightened . . . "

Costa nodded. "The woman says his

clothes are still here. But the bedroom window was open — if he slipped away, that part is my fault." He shoved the lighters back in his pockets and sucked his teeth, frowning. "I have men searching — and they've been told not to harm him if it can be avoided. I think" — he hesitated then seemed to make up his mind — "yes, I have to go back to where it happened. It is not pleasant, Inez. But if you and Senhor Gaunt wish to come . . . "

"*Por favor* . . . if it might help." She glanced at Gaunt and looked relieved when he nodded. But that left another problem. "Anna . . . "

"Is still in the house," confirmed Costa. "I will leave some men here, men who know Luis — he might come back." He glanced quickly at his wrist-watch and grimaced. "If we go now, we will be there before the headquarters people arrive. And Doctor Sollas will be waiting."

"Sollas?" Gaunt showed his surprise.

"Someone had to identify them," said Costa grimly. "Believe me, it was not too easy."

They went by police car. It was a short ride, which ended on a quiet side road on another of the hill slopes which looked down towards Claras. An old Ford station wagon was there with its nearside wheels on the grass verge and the driver's door hanging open. Other vehicles were parked nearby, headlights blazing and with several men standing beside them.

Leaving the police car, Sergeant Costa led the way. He nodded to a uniformed sergeant with a machine-pistol who came to meet them then stopped a few paces away from the Ford and glanced at Inez, then at the uniformed man.

"The lady will stay here, I think," he said quietly. "Senhor Gaunt . . . "

They left Inez with the other sergeant and went on. As they reached the Ford's open door, Gaunt tightened his lips. A blanket had been draped over the front seats, but a woman's feet protruded from one edge, shoeless.

Silently, Costa lifted one edge of the blanket. John Marsh and his wife lay across each other inside the station wagon, dumped there in macabre fashion.

"We have to wait for the forensic experts from Lisbon," said Costa in sober apology. "But — well, see for yourself."

He brought a torch from his pocket and clicked on the beam. For a moment Gaunt felt his stomach heave, then he fought the feeling down and moved closer.

Preston's nephew had been stabbed at least once in the chest. But the bloodied shirt-front was nothing compared with the way his head had been smashed in, shattered like some discarded eggshell.

He glanced at Costa, nodded, and the torch-beam shifted.

Sarah Marsh lay face down, half on top of her husband. There was more blood, and a deep slash wound across one arm showed how she'd fought for life. Again it hadn't stopped there — that long, blonde hair was almost unrecognisably matted with blood from blows which had smashed through her skull to expose the white of brain tissue.

Mercifully, Costa switched off the torch

and lowered the blanket.

"Well?" asked Costa softly. "What kind of man would do such a thing?"

Gaunt could only shake his head.

Looking round, Costa beckoned at one of the shadowy figures and snapped an order. The man he'd summoned brought over a canvas-covered bundle and unwrapped a thick wooden stake. Stains of blood and strands of hair still adhered to one end.

"And the cigarette lighter?" asked Gaunt.

"On the ground, beside the *gasolina* filler pipe — the cap was removed." Costa kicked a loose pebble along the ground, clipping his words to hide his own feelings. "If we assume it was Luis and that he had a knife, then perhaps we can also assume that these people had become lost, saw him, and merely stopped to ask the way."

"So he killed them?"

"I have to shape a picture — but does that mean I like it?" Costa's bitterness came through, then he firmed his lips again. "There are signs Marsh was killed beside the car. There are other signs that his wife tried to run. After — after the killer caught her, he used the stake to make sure then dragged them back here and tried to set the car on fire." He shrugged. "Maybe what is left of his mind decided a fire would burn it all away — except that the cigarette lighter wouldn't work. It was bone dry."

They went back to Inez. Two more figures had joined her at the roadside, a grim-faced Arthur Sollas who looked bulkier than ever in a loose anorak jacket and Bernard Ryan, whose prematurely white hair framed his head like a halo in the weak moonlight. Greetings amounted to nods.

Costa took time off to light a cigarette, looked grimly at his lighter for a moment, then tucked it away and faced them.

"You know how these people were found," he said quietly. "We have been operating extra patrols on roads like this because of petty crime in the area. But I will go over again what little else we know. Doctor Sollas, you were at your villa?"

"Correct," rumbled Sollas, nodding. "With Martin Lawson — we were tidying some paperwork. I left him back there."

"He's probably having kittens by now," murmured Ryan. "Locking the doors and barring windows" — he stopped, glanced at Inez, shrugged apologetically and finished weakly — "well, you know what I mean."

Costa eyed him frostily. "And where were you, Senhor Ryan?"

"In Lisbon, as I told you," answered the photographer wearily. "Pereira drove me in this afternoon, to collect some equipment. Then — well, as a foreman he's maybe more muscle than brain but he knows a few places." He grinned self-consciously. "We drank for a spell, then headed back to the Castelo. The watchman was still helping us unload at the site when you *policia* arrived."

"And the watchman says he saw nothing and heard nothing unusual tonight." Costa gave a heavy sigh. "Which leaves the station wagon. Doctor Sollas?"

"If I've got to repeat everything," growled Sollas with a momentary ill temper. "Marsh and his wife were prowling around the villa, doing nothing but complain." He shot a glance at Gaunt. "You know what they were like — so when they said they wanted to drive into Claras I said they could take the Ford. Where they went after they left . . . " He shrugged.

"They did go to Claras," said Costa, his sallow face impassive. "They were seen around the cafés. But afterwards . . . ?"

"They took a wrong turning," suggested Ryan laconically. He shivered a little in the cold night air. "Hell, this place is in the middle of nowhere, and that pair were the kind who could get lost crossing a road."

Costa didn't find it amusing. But before he could answer a shout from one of the police guards drew his attention to headlights coming fast along the road towards them.

"Headquarters." He pursed his lips. "Senhor Gaunt, it would be better if you took Inez home now." Turning to her he added softly, "Believe me, if anything happens you will be first to hear."

★ ★ ★

225

The same police car took them back to the bungalow. Once there, the uniformed driver came round to help Inez out, gave a formal salute, then climbed back aboard the car and drove away. But another car was still parked on the driveway, its lights out, and as Gaunt went with Inez towards the house an armed policeman watched impassively from the black shadow of a clump of shrubbery.

Maintaining an outward calm, she found her key and opened the front door. But once they were inside and the door had closed again she turned to face Gaunt and tried to speak with lips that, for the moment, could only tremble.

He put a comforting arm round her shoulders and she came in close, hiding her face against his chest. When she did look up, the trembling had stopped but she still wasn't far removed from tears.

"Luis couldn't have killed them," she said with a tired but determined conviction. "I don't care how it looks to Manuel Costa — he couldn't. And Anna said — " she stopped, her eyes widening " — Anna! I'd forgotten about Anna!"

She left Gaunt in the hallway and hurried towards the kitchen. A moment later he heard her voice then the other woman's lower, hesitant reply. The conversation in the kitchen went on for several minutes before Inez left the housekeeper and returned alone.

"Could she help?" asked Gaunt quietly.

"No." Inez shook her head slowly and wearily. "All she knows is the police had her check through the kitchen, to see if there was any kind of knife missing."

"And was there?"

"No." Her lips tightened. "So they said he must have got it somewhere else."

"What about earlier, before he went to bed?"

"He was just — just as usual. Anna says he watched some television and looked at some picture books Francis Preston gave him." She moistened her lips, keeping a veneer of control over her voice. "Anna even thought he looked happier than she'd seen him for weeks . . . "

"They'll find him," said Gaunt, lost for anything else to say. "Manuel Costa won't let him come to harm."

"And afterwards?" She looked at him steadily for a moment. "You're like Manuel. You think Luis killed them."

Gaunt shook his head. "I haven't said that, Inez. But I know Costa's doing his job the best way he can."

"And you've tried to help." She sighed and nodded. "But it's late — there's nothing more you can do for now."

"I'll stay if you like," he suggested quietly.

"*Obrigado* . . . but no, Jonathan." Her mouth shaped a small smile of thanks. "I'll be better alone."

He nodded his understanding, took her hands, and kissed her gently on the lips. Then he turned and went out.

The old Fiat was still where he'd left it that afternoon. Climbing aboard, he took a last glance back at the house then started the car and set it moving.

★ ★ ★

It was after three a.m. when he got back to Claras and the Hotel Da Gama was in darkness, the front door firmly

228

locked. Gaunt rang the night bell, heard it peal somewhere inside, and eventually the door was opened by the desk clerk, who wore an old coat over his pyjamas and was yawning.

He thanked the man, left him muttering and locking the door again, and caught himself yawning in turn as he climbed the stairs to his room. Going in, he switched on the light, tensed for an instant as he realised someone was already there — then relaxed with a grunt of irritation as he saw it was Jaime. "What the hell do you want this time?" demanded Gaunt brusquely.

"*Tenho* . . . I am looking for help, Senhor Gaunt." The young, dark-haired hotel porter sat up in the chair where he'd been dozing, rubbed his eyes and grinned uneasily.

"Not from me," said Gaunt shortly, and thumbed towards the door. "Out — it can keep till morning."

"*Por favor* . . . please, Senhor Gaunt." Jaime got to his feet, a worried earnestness in his voice. "This is too important, believe me."

"Believing you is something I'd worry

about." Gaunt peeled off his jacket, dropped it on the bed, then sighed. "All right — keep it short."

Jaime licked his lips. "The police are looking for Luis Torres — I know where he is."

Gaunt froze, staring at him.

"A friend and I have him hidden," declared Jaime quickly. "But it can only be for tonight — we need help to get him somewhere safer."

Gaunt rubbed a slow, confused hand across his forehead. "Jaime, do you know why they're searching for him?"

"*Sim*. They say he killed two people." Jaime combined a crude noise and gesture to his own opinion clear. "They're the crazy ones."

"Start at the beginning," suggested Gaunt, cloaking a grin. "When did you find him — and where?"

"Maybe an hour ago. My friend Rodrigues and I — uh" — Jaime hesitated, eyeing him cautiously — "we went for a walk."

"At two a.m.?" Gaunt raised an incredulous eyebrow.

"We planned to catch rabbits." The

youngster's innocent dark eyes met his own. "There is good money in rabbits, senhor."

"And even better money other ways."

"Senhor?" Jaime blinked.

Gaunt stuck a cigarette in his mouth, lit it, and sat down on the bed. "Sergeant Costa's been chasing his tail trying to catch a couple of small-time burglars who operate late at night. But I suppose you wouldn't know anything about that?"

"Of course not, senhor." Jamie shook his head and quickly switched the subject. "But, like I said, we were walking outside the village when we heard something moving behind a hedge an' we thought it was maybe a rabbit. Instead, it was Luis Torres — and we had brought him back here before we heard what had happened."

"Here? You mean . . . "

Jaime nodded. "He's in this hotel, senhor."

Gaunt swallowed. "He didn't give any trouble?"

"Trouble?" Jaime gave him an almost pitying look. "He was frightened, maybe. But he knows us — and he was tired and cold, wearing only pyjamas." He paused hopefully. "You will help us, Senhor Gaunt?"

Gaunt shook his head.

"But" — Jaime's mouth fell open — "but you are a friend of his sister . . . "

"I'm still not crazy enough to risk spending the next few years living on fish stew in a Portuguese jail," said Gaunt grimly. "Not without a damned good reason, anyway. If you want to do Luis Torres a favour, you'll turn him over to Sergeant Costa. Nothing else makes sense — for Torres or anyone."

"I thought . . . "

"You thought wrong. He needs care — special care," said Gaunt wearily. "Could you give him it, do you know anyone else who will?"

Silenced, Jaime looked down at the floor.

"So I'll see him, then I'll contact Sergeant Costa," Gaunt told him, getting up from the bed. "We'll think of some kind of story that keeps you out of it."

They went out of the room, down one flight of stairs, and stopped at a bedroom door. Jaime knocked lightly and waited, knocked again then, frowning, tried the handle. The door opened a fraction and he looked into the darkened room then hesitated, looking at Gaunt uneasily.

Pushing him aside, Gaunt opened the door wide and found the light switch. The overhead bulb which flared to life showed a figure lying sprawled on the floor. He heard a gasp of alarm from Jaime but ignored him, going over to kneel beside a youth about the same age. His eyes were closed and there was a trickle of drying blood on his forehead. But he was breathing, and whoever had done it had stopped long enough to take a pillow from the bed and put it under his head.

"He's all right," Gaunt assured Jaime, who was still standing nervously in the doorway. "Knocked out, that's all. Get some water."

While Jaime obeyed, filling a jug from the room washbasin, Gaunt glanced around and saw an old-fashioned chamber-pot lying on its side on the carpet. His lips twisted in a grin. A blow from that kind of heavy pottery could have been lethal — if the user had tried hard enough.

"Senhor . . . " Jaime brought over the jug.

Taking it, Gaunt carefully poured a stream of water on the other youth's face. It brought a groan then a splutter and he stopped as Rodrigues propped himself up on his elbows, squinting painfully in the light.

"Was it Luis who hit you?" asked Gaunt.

A nod and grimace was answer enough.

"But why?" asked Jaime, bewildered. "Why wouldn't he stay?"

"Ever tried to hold a wild bird in your hand?" asked Gaunt softly. "All it has is instinct — and that's Luis."

They stared at him, trying to understand.

He called the *policia* station from a telephone in the hotel lobby and left a message for Costa that Luis Torres had been seen in Claras. Then he called Inez and told her the same, plus a little more.

There were enough men out searching, men who knew the country around and to whom a stranger would be little more than an additional liability. The best kind of help he could give, he decided, might come later with morning.

Going back to his room, he got out of his clothes and saw the bottle of painkillers waiting. But this once, he felt too tired to even need them.

Dropping on the bed, he slept till well after dawn.

7

MORNING came warm and bright, accompanied by the strident siren of a police car as it crossed the cobbled square below Gaunt's bedroom. He heard other sirens as he yawned awake and dressed and when he looked out still another car was turning into the side street that led to the *policia* post, watched by several interested groups of bystanders.

There was no sign of Jaime when he went down to the dining room and an attempt at conversation with the plump, dull-faced Portuguese girl who brought him breakfast foundered quickly. Giving up, Gaunt gulped some coffee, left the rest, and went out of the hotel, crossing the sunlit cobbles and past the gushing fountain while curious eyes watched him in silence.

Inside the *policia* post the main office was busy with new faces — police with clipped city accents who seemed equally

236

busy shouting down telephones and at each other. But one of the regular Claras constables came over and greeted him warily.

"*Por favor*, where can I find Sergeant Costa?" asked Gaunt.

"At the Torres' place, Senhor Gaunt." The man thumbed wryly at the turmoil behind him and lowered his voice. "He told me he would try to stay away till this circus quietens."

Gaunt grimaced his sympathy. "Any trace of Luis Torres yet?"

A slow headshake was answer enough, then the man was called away.

Pensively, Gaunt left the post and returned across the square to where he'd parked the Fiat. He was still thinking about Luis Torres as he climbed aboard and started the car. A chill night in the open might be a minimal hardship for an ordinary man, but how would it leave a sickly, bewildered, inadequately clad fugitive like Inez's brother?

He caught himself contrasting that picture against another, the battered, bleeding bodies of John and Sarah Marsh left thrown together in their car. In life, they'd been easy to dislike — but that faded against the savage death which had come their way.

Had it been Torres? The tendril of doubt in his mind had grown considerably with a night's sleep. Because, hazy as it might be, there was a frightening alternative, one that went straight back to the whole chain of doubt and suspicion which surrounded the Castelo de Rosa digging site.

If only that in itself made sense — Gaunt shook his head. Any of the alleged ghosts lurking around the old Moorish watch-tower must be enjoying a grim belly-laugh at it all.

From Claras, he drove straight out to the Torres bungalow. A police car was leaving as he arrived, the driver sitting stiffly behind the wheel and a solitary, high-ranking officer scowling in the back seat. Tyres spattering gravel, it swung off in the direction of the hills in a fast-moving plume of dust.

Shrugging, Gaunt turned in towards the driveway and was promptly flagged down by a constable with a rifle slung over one shoulder. But it was one of

Costa's men, and he was waved on towards the house.

Parking outside, Gaunt walked across to the porch steps then saw the door was lying open and heard voices coming from inside. The voices stopped as he rang the doorbell, then, after a moment, Inez appeared in the hallway. She was in a plain blue denim shirt tucked into matching trousers, her face was bare of make-up and she looked as if she'd had little sleep. But she managed a small, tight smile of welcome.

"I hoped you'd come," she said simply.

"You should have known I would." He thumbed past her. "Sergeant Costa?"

"Yes — a police captain from Lisbon is in charge now." Her lips tightened. "He just left. Compared with him, Manuel is a beginner."

She led him through to the front room. Eyes red rimmed, a stubble of beard darkening his cheeks, Sergeant Costa sat sprawled in an armchair under the *fado* portrait. His greeting amounted to a gloomy wave of a hand. There were mud-stains on his shoes, his clothes were crumpled, and an ashtray beside him was choked with old cigarette ends.

"If I was paid by the kilometre for last night I'd be a rich man, Senhor Gaunt," he said wearily, as if reading Gaunt's mind. "Headquarters may have sent us all kinds of damned experts and bosses, but people like me still get left with the donkey-work."

"It's that kind of world — too many chiefs but a shortage of Indians," agreed Gaunt dryly. Inez went over to a side board and poured him a cup of coffee from a bubbling percolator. As she brought the cup over, he asked Costa, "You still think it was Luis?"

Costa shrugged awkwardly. "Have I any choice?" For a moment he avoided looking at Inez, frowning to himself. "First, we have to find him. The way he showed up at your hotel last night puzzles me — why would he go there?"

"He was seen, then he vanished again," said Gaunt neutrally, sipping the coffee. "That's all I know."

"Seen by Jaime." Costa treated the point like a bad smell, then sighed. "Inez, now that our so efficient captain from headquarters has gone, maybe we could try . . . "

"No, not again, Manuel!" She cut him short angrily, her small fists clenched. "Can't you understand? I've told you every place I can think he might go. I want him found too, for his own sake."

"I know that," soothed Costa. He scrubbed a hopeful thumb along his stubbled chin. "That coffee — uh — smells good."

She glared at him then, still tight-faced, went back to the sideboard and poured another cup. Costa murmured his thanks as she brought it over, took a gulp, then glanced at Gaunt.

"Every man we have searched the hills most of the night. They started again at dawn, with dogs — and if that doesn't work, some army men may be brought in to help." He scowled at the floor, "The way I feel doesn't matter, Senhor Gaunt. He has to be found."

"That part I'll go along with," said Gaunt grimly. "But what about the rest of it?"

"Eh?" Costa didn't understand.

"I can remember when a certain

humble sergeant of detectives had other ideas," declared Gaunt icily. "What about Pereira?"

"Now?" Costa gestured his impatience. "He can wait — if he ever mattered."

"Pereira?" Inez looked at them, bewildered. "The foreman at the Castelo site?"

Gaunt nodded.

"Things are different now," muttered Costa uneasily. "Even if Francis Preston's death was murder then . . . " he left it there.

"Luis?" Inez flared at the unspoken inference. "You can't think that — not after what you told me!"

"About the time of death?" Costa grimaced miserably. "That calculation is always part guesswork. Inez, when it comes to decisions we have to act on what we know — not what some medical examiner thinks might be right." He drew a deep breath, then turned on Gaunt. "And one thing I do know, one thing you might remember, Senhor Gaunt. If Marsh and his wife had not been excited by your crazy story of lost treasure and rewards they would have gone back to

England yesterday. They would be alive — none of this would have happened."

It was true, though Gaunt hadn't thought of it that way before. He flushed, a retort ready on his lips. But Inez stepped between them.

"Two grown men — or supposed to be." She eyed them angrily. "Stop it — it doesn't help anyone."

Manuel Costa looked sheepish then slowly shook his head. "Senhor Gaunt . . . "

"Forget it," said Gaunt, "We've all got problems." He remembered one of his own. "Inez I want to make a telephone call to Lisbon. It won't take long."

She led him through to her bedroom. It was small and neat and pink, with the telephone on a bedside table. Once she'd gone, Gaunt dialled the British Embassy number, waited while it rang out then, when the switchboard answered, asked for the duty officer and gave his name. This time he was connected without delay.

"Gaunt?" The embassy man's voice crackled briskly over the line. "I'll save you time. We've had a report from the Portuguese about Preston's relatives being murdered. Usual expressions of regret to the ambassador and that sort of thing. Still, they seem to know who killed them, which is the main thing. Have they caught him yet?"

"No, they're still looking." Gaunt answered him woodenly.

"Well, we'll take care of any formalities from this end — not your problem, eh?" The duty officer dismissed the matter. "But talking of problems, what the hell did you get involved in last night?"

"Meaning?" Gaunt frowned at the mouthpiece.

"Two separate inquiries asking if we knew anything about you — one from the local NATO security people, the other from a more discreet Portuguese government contact." The voice in his ear gave a mock tut of disapproval. "We said you were clean, of course, and that seemed to satisfy them. But — ah . . . "

"Some small-time thugs tried to mug me last night, that's all." Gaunt smiled grimly. It sounded as if a certain U.S. Navy lieutenant left nothing to chance.

"Oh." The duty officer sounded

disappointed. "That's all right then. But . . . "

Gaunt cut him short. "What about that check I wanted on Lawson and Ryan?"

"Your two digging site friends?" There was a slight pause and he heard a rustle of papers. "Yes, we got a little, some of it interesting. Martin Lawson seems all right, but dull — he came here from Spain about a year ago after a spell as a university lecturer in Madrid. But your photographer gentleman, Bernard Ryan, sounds worth watching."

"Why?" Gaunt tensed hopefully.

"He was on the sticky end of some North African gun-running a few years back. Never did get caught, but he knew some unpleasant people — I got that from our own security people. The Portuguese say he's clean."

"Thanks," said Gaunt gratefully. "It could matter."

"I owed you a favour," protested the duty officer cheerfully. "Today's *Financial Times*. Gaunt — Consolidated Breweries down two points to 122. Malters another five up at 165. Going

245

well for us both, eh?"

"You bought in?" He asked it in a dull voice, guessing the answer.

"A thousand Malters — I emptied the piggy bank." The embassy man hesitated with slight embarrassment. "How high would you let them ride? I mean, when's best to sell?"

"Now."

"Eh?But . . . "

"You bought the wrong damned company," snarled Gaunt, hung up on a squeak of protest and closed his eyes for a moment.

The Consolidated bid for Malters was real enough. But the real tip, the one that mattered, had been given to him by a douce Edinburgh spinster who had been the long-ago mistress of a Scandinavian beer baron. Their ardour might have died down to mere pen-friend letters, but the Edinburgh spinster lived well.

And while the Consolidated cat was busy trying to swallow the Malters mouse a certain European consortium of brewers were going to grab Consolidated by the tail. When that happened, the Malters price would collapse overnight.

But Consolidated's shares should start flying.

★ ★ ★

He was only thinking about Bernard Ryan when he went back to Inez and Costa. The tall, prematurely white-haired photographer, so friendly and easy-going, had seemed an unlikely candidate.

Except that Ryan had taken his photograph at the site, that the men who had jumped him at the casino might have had more than the make of car he was driving to help identify him — and that Ryan was Carlos Pereira's rock-solid alibi for the previous night.

"Senhor Gaunt, I must ask a favour." Sergeant Costa was on his feet, still looking sheepish but apparently ready to leave. "*Por favor* . . . I need a lift." Costa grinned his embarrassment. "The headquarters captain has my car. It would not take long, I promise."

Gaunt glanced at Inez.

"I'm going to stay here," she declared. "That way, if there is news . . . "

"All right." He nodded his understanding.

"I'll come back later, once I've seen a couple of people." A thought struck him. "Inez, you said Preston gave Luis some books. Could you look them out while I'm gone?" He ignored Costa's caustic sniff and added some encouragement. "They might matter."

"I will. It will give me something to do," she said quietly.

* * *

It had been cool inside the house, but back in the open the sky was cloudless blue and the temperature was rising. The shrubbery had come alive with buzzing insects and the sun was warm on Gaunt's back as he walked with Costa towards the Fiat.

"Don't you want to know where we're going, Senhor Gaunt?" asked Costa with a peeved irritation.

"If you feel like telling." Gaunt stopped and stuck his hands in his pockets. "But suppose we settle one thing first, Sergeant. I didn't come uninvited into this mess — you talked me into it at the beginning."

"True." Gloomily, Costa kicked a stray pebble and scowled. "So I have only myself to blame?"

"Something like that."

"*Obrigado* . . . " Costa managed a thawing grimace. "Well, first I have to collect the Marshes' car and take it into Claras. The forensic people from headquarters are finished with it, and as usual the locals are left to tidy up. But afterwards — yes, maybe you are right. Maybe Carlos Pereira deserves more attention. I could begin by talking to the watchman at the Castelo digging site." Suddenly, a touch of his old, lazy humour slipped through. "Could I impose on you to come along?"

"Sergeant, you're beginning to make sense again." Gaunt grinned and brought out the Fiat's keys. "Sense enough to do the driving, anyway."

They got aboard, and Costa struggled to adjust the driving seat.

"No prize for guessing a long-legged Scottish giraffe has been using this," he complained, finishing the job and putting on his sunglasses.

"And now a short-ass Portuguese

peasant has his turn," countered Gaunt easily. It was hot inside the Fiat, and he wound down the passenger window as Costa started the car moving. "Sergeant, if you meant what you said about Pereira maybe I can help a little."

Costa gave a quick glance of interest, but Gaunt waited till they'd passed the guard at the bottom of the driveway and were travelling on the road. Then he gave a quick summary of most of what he knew, including the embassy information on Ryan.

When he'd finished, Costa gave a puzzled but appreciative whistle then rubbed a hand along the steering wheel's rim, leaving a momentary streak of perspiration.

"*Obrigado* again, Senhor Gaunt, and this time I mean it." He frowned at the road ahead, then blew the horn briefly as they passed a farm cart drawn by an undersized donkey. "Finding Luis still matters most to me, for obvious reasons. But if I can produce one firm reason why he could not have killed these people then — then will I happily spit in a certain *policia* captain's face!"

Suddenly, he began humming confidently to himself. Glancing at him, Gaunt said nothing but recognised the signs. Sergeant Costa felt he had something worth while to do again. But as the car purred on along the dry, dusty road, scrub and cactus alternating with almond trees in blossom and an occasional, rocky slope terraced for vines, Gaunt wished he could share the man's confidence.

To believe that all that had happened had to centre on the Castelo de Rosa site was one thing. To make sense of it was another until something emerged to act as a catalyst, and until then how much could they really do?

* * *

It took about ten minutes to reach the farm road where the Ford station wagon had been found. It hadn't been moved and a constable with a rifle slung from one shoulder was still on guard, his pedal cycle propped against a fence.

Costa spoke to him briefly, then led the way over to the station wagon. Inside, the bloodstains on the seats and carpets had been covered in plastic sheeting and a mist of grey fingerprint powder had been sprayed over everything. Opening the driver's door, Costa snorted his disgust and flicked a hand at the flies buzzing around inside.

"Did they find anything?" asked Gaunt.

Costa shook his head. "Nothing that mattered — not even a decent fingerprint from the steering wheel and the *gasolina* filler cap was the same." Climbing aboard, he checked the foot pedals, sighed, and brought the seat forward. "If you follow me back to Claras, then once I am finished, we can go straight to the Castelo site."

"I'll meet you at the site but I've something else to do first," Gaunt stifled the incipient protest. "I'm only taking a drive across to Sollas's villa. A few words there might help stir things up."

"*Quanto* . . . by how much?" queried Costa bleakly, leaning forward to key-start the Ford. "Already we have all the trouble we can handle."

"Then I'll stir gently," promised Gaunt.

Grunting, Costa let in the clutch. Gaunt watched him struggle to turn the big station wagon on the narrow road then, as it drew away and began travelling back down the road towards Claras he smiled and lit a cigarette. The policeman who had been on guard nodded at him, mounted his bicycle, and solemnly pedalled off in the same direction.

Left alone, Gaunt stayed for a moment looking at the tyre marks on the grass and a small patch of sump oil, all that remained of what had happened. Then he shrugged, went back to the Fiat, and set it moving.

★ ★ ★

A mud-streaked jeep from the digging site was the only vehicle parked outside Arthur Sollas's villa. Gaunt stopped the Fiat beside it, got out, and went over to the house. He rang the bell twice before the door swung open, and then it was Martin Lawson who peered out at him.

"Oh." The bald, chubby archaeologist blinked at him then stepped back. "Come in, Mr Gaunt. I thought — well, I thought it might be the police." He

253

gestured vaguely to two closed and labelled suitcases lying in the hallway. "They said they'd collect the Marshes' belongings."

Gaunt entered and Lawson closed the door, still shaking his head over the suitcases.

"We packed them this morning. An ordeal on its own, Mr Gaunt. With Frank Preston, it was sad. But Marsh and his wife were so much younger — and to be killed so brutally . . . " He let it tail away. "Has Torres been captured yet?"

"No." Gaunt wondered if the visit was going to turn out a waste of time. "Where's Doctor Sollas?"

"At the site, I think. He left to go there, anyway." Lawson tutted to himself. "In fact, I'm on my own." Then he brightened. "I've some coffee brewed if you'd like a cup."

"Thanks." Gaunt followed him through to a large, untidy kitchen. A brown metal percolator was on the stove and Lawson fussed around. At last, he brought over two steaming mugs and handed one to Gaunt.

"There" — he beamed nervously,

nursing his own — "now, can I help?"

Gaunt shrugged. "The embassy at Lisbon said that as I was here I could take care of a few formalities for them — British nationals killed abroad, the usual reports." He saw Lawson nod wisely, and went on. "You were here with Doctor Sollas when Marsh and his wife took the car?"

"That's right." Lawson rubbed his chin nervously. "They were — ah — restless and wanted to do something, almost anything. Not being able to find any trace of Preston's Treasure Trove expedition had — ah — upset them."

"I can imagine," said Gaunt dryly. "But they didn't say where they were going?"

"Just into Claras." Lawson frowned a little, "The police know all this."

"The embassy like their own paperwork," soothed Gaunt. "So you were here with Doctor Sollas. But Ryan was with Pereira?"

"Yes." An embarrassed smile crossed the other man's round face and he shifted his feet awkwardly. "Bernard didn't really need to go with Pereira, of course, but it was an excuse to get away for the evening. And by then Marsh and his wife were — well, it had become rather a strain. Bernard isn't particularly good at hiding his feelings."

"I've noticed." Gaunt took a gulp of the coffee, but shook his head at the offer of a sandwich. "It's been a bad week for you people. You knew Preston fairly well, didn't you?"

"We'd met," said Lawson uneasily. "I couldn't say I knew him, Mr Gaunt. I — well, I suppose it was luck he remembered my name and that I was out here."

"Just luck?"

Lawson look puzzled. "I don't understand."

"Then let's see if I can help," said Gaunt softly, laying down his mug. "Georges Salvador told Preston he was on a sure thing if he excavated at the Castelo." He saw the way Lawson's expression froze, and knew he'd guessed right. "Salvador wouldn't know that on his own. Someone had to tell him — an expert. Someone like you, Lawson."

"Me?" Lawson licked his lips. "I hardly know Senhor Salvador . . ."

"That's not what I asked," murmured Gaunt. As Lawson tried to look away he grabbed him by the shoulder and brought him round again. "You told him, didn't you?"

Reluctantly, Lawson nodded then swallowed hard. "I — yes, I heard he was interested in Claras, and I'd come across a mention of the site. But . . ."

"As long as you got paid," said Gaunt cynically. "Does Doctor Sollas know?"

Lawson shook his head.

"That part isn't my business," Gaunt told him curtly. "But last night is. What happened here after Marsh and his wife left?"

"Nothing. I — I went to bed."

Gaunt frowned. "What about Sollas?"

"I don't know." Lawson gestured feebly. "I was asleep — but he woke me when the police came to tell us what had happened."

Gaunt considered him silently for a moment then gave a fractional nod. Marsh and his wife had left the villa

257

about ten p.m., their bodies had been found around one a.m. — three hours of suddenly unaccounted time against Arthur Sollas's name.

He left Lawson in the kitchen and returned through the villa to the front door. But when he stepped out onto the porch he stopped short. Georges Salvador's blue Jaguar was parked beside the Fiat, and Salvador stood at the foot of the porch steps smiling up at him with all the cold-eyed interest of a hungry fox.

Salvador wasn't alone. Leaning against the Fiat, cleaning his nails with the tip of a long-bladed knife, Carlos Pereira presented a picture of stocky, studied but watchful disinterest.

"We seem fated to meet, Senhor Gaunt," said Salvador softly. "What brought you here? More curiosity?"

"Something like that." Gaunt shrugged and came down the steps. "Lawson's inside, if you want him."

"*Obrigado*, but he can wait," murmured Salvador. He signalled with a forefinger and Pereira began ambling over, still using the knife. "I offered you some advice last night, Senhor Gaunt, and a second chance."

"I remember." Gaunt nodded indifferently. "The answer stays the same."

"Then you're a fool." The smile died.

"Maybe." Glancing at Pereira, who was still using the knife-tip on his nails, Gaunt grimaced a little. "How long since your little friend joined the payroll?"

"We have an arrangement," said Salvador bleakly. "He protects certain of my investments."

"Nice for you," murmured Gaunt. "But I'd rather buy a large-sized dog — you can trust dogs. And they don't play with knives like they'd just been invented."

Pereira froze, his pock-marked face shaping a snarl. But Salvador gave a fractional, restraining headshake.

"He knows exactly how to use a knife," said Salvador softly. "I would advise you to take my word for that."

"If you say so," Gaunt let his right hand stray into his pocket, where the lead-filled truncheon was waiting. He gripped it and brought it out into view, the short tip still just inside his pocket flap. "Just make sure

259

he doesn't get any ideas about a practical demonstration — because I'd take you first."

Salvador hesitated, glancing with guarded contempt at the little truncheon. Then the decision was taken for him as the villa door clicked open behind them. Martin Lawson came out onto the porch and stopped there, an uncertain smile on his face.

"More visitors for you," said Gaunt grimly.

"I — uh — I thought I heard voices." Lawson bobbed his head anxiously. "Come in, Senhor Salvador — you too, Carlos."

"I can recommend the coffee," said Gaunt, keeping his eyes on Salvador but letting the truncheon slide back into his pocket. "Go ahead. You'll have things to talk about."

Tight-lipped, Salvador nodded. Smiling a little, Gaunt stepped past him and brought one heel hard down on Pereira's instep.

"Clumsy," said Gaunt apologetically above the foreman's yelp of pain. "I keep doing things like that."

He walked over to the Fiat without looking back.

* * *

A few minutes later he was pulling up at the main gate of the Castelo de Rosa site. When he honked the horn the gate opened and he drove through, to stop beside the huts. A police car was parked there, its driver behind the wheel, while Sergeant Costa was standing outside the nearest hut talking with Arthur Sollas and a small, nut-brown man in a coarse wool shirt and old corduroy jeans.

"You again?" Arthur Sollas scowled as he joined them. "Gaunt, you may be doing your job, but you're beginning to get on my nerves the way you turn up every time there's trouble."

"Here?" Gaunt raised an innocent eyebrow. "What's happened now?"

"*Pequeno* . . . a small thing." Sergeant Costa gave him a quick look which might have killed then cleared his throat uncomfortably. "Doctor Sollas dislikes certain questions I have been asking . . . "

"Dislikes?" Sollas grated the word. "You're wasting time, Costa. Why don't you get back to where you belong, chasing that damned killer Luis Torres?" He switched his glare to Gaunt. "Or was this your idea?"

"Doctor, I don't know what the hell you're talking about," declared Gaunt sadly. He thumbed at the other man, who stood with an expression of gloomy boredom on his thin, unshaven weasel face. "Who's this?

"Pracard, our night watchman," snapped Sollas. "Costa seems to imagine he's lying."

"The night watchman?" Gaunt considered the little man with a new interest. "The same one you had the night Preston was killed?"

"No." Sollas kept his temper with an effort. "I fired that idiot. Pracard took over — Ryan dug him up from somewhere."

"More buried treasure." Gaunt nodded solemnly.

"And all I have asked is if he is sure he saw nothing last night," said Sergeant Costa wearily. "That and if he remembers the exact time Senhor Ryan arrived. The details are necessary — headquarters demand a full report on the movements of everyone who knew Senhor Marsh and his wife." He gestured defensively. "When Senhor Ryan was here, he didn't seem to mind."

"Where's Ryan anyway?" queried Gaunt, glancing around.

"Gone back to work," said Sollas sourly. "We're still trying to keep things ticking over. Placard" — he turned to the watchman — "is there anything at all you can tell the sergeant?"

"*Nao*, Doctor Sollas." The watchman shook his head wearily.

"That's what I'd expect." Sollas pointed an angry hand towards the wooded hills. "There's a homicidal maniac running loose out there, Costa. I'll warn you now, if Torres shows up here again . . . "

"Again?" interrupted Gaunt, surprised.

Costa shrugged, unconvinced. "Two of the workmen on the site thought they saw someone among the trees this morning."

"So we went looking for him, and we didn't go empty-handed," rumbled Sollas grimly. "If he turns up again, we'll shoot on sight."

"Do that, and I'll arrest every man involved," countered Sergeant Costa, flushing. "You're talking about a man, not an animal."

"Then if he matters so much you'd better find him first." Bleakly Sollas dismissed the watchman with a nod then swung to face them again as the man left. "Finished, Sergeant?"

"*Sim*, for now." Not troubling to hide his spluttering fury, Costa added for Gaunt's benefit, "If I am needed, the *policia* post at Claras can contact me."

He strode off to the police car, climbed aboard, and slammed the passenger door shut. Starting up, the car shot away and vanished out through the gates.

"Which leaves you." Hitching his thumbs into the waistband of his slacks, Arthur Sollas considered Gaunt with ill-concealed impatience. "What do you want?"

"I've a puzzle of my own to solve," said Gaunt mildly. He looked around the site for a moment, noting the very few men who seemed to be working,

264

then combed a hand through his rumpled mop of hair. "I thought maybe you could help."

"If it's still that damned Treasure Trove nonsense, don't waste my time," warned Sollas, bristling. "Not after what's happened."

"There's still a lot of money involved in it," mused Gaunt. "Enough to make a reasonable motive for murder — if it hadn't been Luis Torres the police were after." He took out a cigarette and lit it carefully, not looking at the man. "And things aren't always how they seem. Even alibis . . ."

"Meaning?"

Gaunt shrugged. "Do I have to spell it out, Doctor? Take your own case. Lawson is your alibi at the villa, but does Sergeant Costa know he was asleep most of the time?"

Arthur Sollas swallowed hard, controlled himself with an effort, then came back with a stabbing fury behind every word.

"If I had your kind of weevil mind I might have a different notion," he snarled, red-faced. "Motive? What about you, Gaunt? I could dream up the idea that maybe you got a lead to your damned Treasure Trove through the Torres girl. Then the idea of backing her claim and getting a share could be a hell of a sight easier if Preston's relatives were eliminated."

"And I could have given her brother that job?" Gaunt treated the suggestion with a wooden respect. "I never thought of it that way." Deliberately, he switched in a new direction. "Doctor, do you know a man in Lisbon named Jose Andella?"

Sollas blinked, rubbed the same finger back across his nose, scowled, and shook his head dangerously.

"You'll find him at the Jeronimos Museum," said Gaunt. "Look him up. He'll tell you the real story about Preston and this site — if you don't know it already."

Open-mouthed, the bulky figure stared at him in what seemed genuine bewilderment.

"Jose Andella," reminded Gaunt softly. "Goodbye, Doctor."

Every step he took towards the Fiat he expected a bellow from Sollas. But he reached it, set it moving — and still the man stood staring as he drove out of the camp.

★ ★ ★

Once the fence and the coral tinted stone of the old Castelo watchtower had been lost along the tree-lined track Gaunt slowed the car and pulled in. Switching off the engine, he slumped back against the stained upholstery, grinned wryly at himself in the rear-view mirror, and took a long draw on what was left of his cigarette.

He'd promised Costa that he'd stir things up — and he'd done it. But how much was it going to achieve?

For a couple of minutes he sat there, trying to force the tangled confusion of it all into some kind of order that made sense. But it didn't happen. If anything, the mess seemed worse than ever.

Giving up, Gaunt stubbed out the cigarette and reached for the starter key. Then he stopped, staring at a thick patch of red-flowered scrub near the track — scrub from which two small black and white birds had just exploded skyward in twittering fright.

A fox, another bird, maybe a deer, half a dozen possible reasons clicked through his mind. But there was still another. Searching for the door handle, he made a deliberate unhurried job of climbing out.

For a long moment he stood beside the car, just listening. The black and white birds were still circling overhead, crickets were sawing away somewhere near, and dried leaves rustled when he shifted his feet. But nothing moved over at the red-flowered scrub.

"Luis?" He waited then tried again, louder. "Luis, you know me — Senhor Gaunt."

There was no wind, but the scrub stirred a little.

"Let's go home, Luis." Gaunt took a slow step forward, then another. Suddenly there was a louder rustle then he had a brief glimpse of a blurred figure moving on the far side of the scrub. Another moment and the figure was running, heading deep into the trees, vanishing from sight.

Gaunt didn't try to follow. A regiment of men could have hidden in that dense, dark woodland and laughed at one man's attempt to find them. He needed help. Either Sergeant Costa's kind of help, which meant uniformed men and dogs. Or the other kind, the kind Luis Torres was more likely to answer.

Going back to the car, Gaunt drove on again. Reaching the main road, he turned right towards Claras and about a kilometre on found a filling station with a pay phone he could use. When he dialled Inez's number she answered within two beats of the ringing tone.

"Are Costa's men still prowling outside?" he asked without preamble.

She gave a small gasp over the line, a mixture of hope and fear. "Have you found Luis?"

"I think I spotted him." Gaunt glanced round in the booth, but the pump attendant was busy with a Volkswagen which had pulled in. "Dream up some kind of story to get away without a fuss. I'm at a filling station just this side of the turn-off for Castelo de Rosa."

"I know it," she said quickly. "Wait for me." And the phone went down.

★ ★ ★

About twenty minutes passed before the open red Lancia came snarling along the road and swung into the filling station. It stopped beside Gaunt, who was finishing a can of beer he'd bought from a self-service dispenser and Inez reached over to open the passenger door.

"You're sure, Jonathan?" she asked as he threw away the can and climbed in.

"No," he said bluntly. "Just that there's something up there — and he ran."

She bit her lip and nodded. "I couldn't come sooner. I didn't want it to look as if I was rushing off."

"What did you tell them?"

Inez twisted a smile. "That I was going into Claras to see Manuel Costa."

"That should hold them, unless he comes looking for you." Gaunt glanced at his watch. It was already past noon, a lot later than he'd expected. "You know the roads around here, Inez. Is there another way we can get near the

270

Castelo site without being spotted?"

"Yes, but it would take time." She rubbed a hand thoughtfully along the thigh seam of her trousers. "We'd have to make a wide circle round the hills."

"Then forget it."

The sudden harsh note in his voice made her stare.

"Why?" she asked.

"We've got to get to him before anyone else does." Gaunt left it at that, glanced at the car's fuel gauge, saw the needle reading almost half full, and made up his mind. "Where you hid the car the last time you went up there will have to do, and . . . " He stopped, staring at the driving seat as if seeing it for the first time.

Inez had it fully forward on the slides. When he'd driven the car, he'd needed the same seat fully back to drive in comfort.

A sudden mental picture of Costa crossed his mind. Costa having to move the Ford station wagon's seat forward before he could reach the pedals properly. Yet, if anything, John Marsh had been smaller than Costa and his wife positively petite by comparison.

Then how could Marsh have driven the Ford?

It would fall down if the station wagon seat had been moved during the fingerprint check. But otherwise — mouth tightening, Gaunt took the thought on. Arthur Sollas was a big man and Bernard Ryan was another member of the Castelo team who must match him in height.

Inez blipped the accelerator with a touch of impatience.

"Let's go," he agreed quietly.

She drove well, with a skilled, unflurried assurance which didn't waste a moment yet kept the car travelling smoothly. Gaunt's first worry began when they left the main road on the secondary route towards the hills, but he was able to relax again when they passed the fork of the Castelo track without meeting other traffic.

Moments later Inez slowed the car, frowning ahead. Then, suddenly, she turned the wheel to the right and they bounced across a strip of rough grassland to stop behind a clump of young trees.

"Here," she said confidently.

Gaunt got out and walked back to the road to check for himself. Satisfied the car wouldn't be seen, he returned to find Inez rummaging in the dashboard glovebox. When she emerged, she was carrying a small pair of binoculars and a small, cloth-wrapped bundle.

"You'd better have these," she said almost hesitantly. "They belonged to Luis, before the accident. I thought — well, I brought them anyway."

Gaunt put the binoculars round his neck by their strap then unwrapped the cloth and gave a mild whistle of surprise. It was a service issue FN self-loading pistol, a nine millimetre automatic only slightly in need of oiling. He checked the pistol, found it still held a full thirteen-round magazine, and stuffed it in his waistband without comment.

"Where now?" he asked.

She led the way, setting a fast pace through the upward slope of undergrowth and trees. In a matter of minutes they were at the edge of the track which led to the Castelo site, waited there a moment to make sure it was clear, and then went across quickly.

From there Gaunt took the lead, working gradually left through the thickening woodland until the blanketing leaves overhead had reduced the sunlight to a dull gloom. When he reckoned they were close to where he'd seen that blurred figure disappearing he called another halt. All around them were the small, living noises of any forest . . . tiny buzzing and rustling noises, the faint sigh of a shifting tree-branch, the distant chuckle of some unseen bird.

But nothing more.

"Anywhere from here on," he said wryly, flicking at a large fly which seemed determined to land on his forehead. "If he's still around, then he'll see us."

"In this?" Inez looked at the dark, shadowy world which surrounded them, something less than hope in her voice. But she nodded and drew a deep breath. "Can I try calling him?"

"Better not." He was glad she didn't ask why.

They set off again, at a slower pace. Twice they came across traces of litter from some long-ago picnic, once a sudden hope ended as an old coat abandoned by some tramp. Then, gradually, the trees began to thin again and in another moment they were looking down towards the little valley of the Castelo site, still bathed in bright sunlight and with its squat stone watchtower standing guardian over the long brown scars of the excavation trenches.

"Far enough." Gaunt sank down among the long grass, glad of a chance to rest, his back already beginning to protest at the prolonged exercise.

More reluctant but still wearily, Inez followed his example and lay face down, her arms pillowing her head. Along the way, her long dark hair had come loose and cascaded around her shoulders, the denim shirt was dark with perspiration against her back, and she already looked as though she'd had enough.

Lighting two cigarettes, Gaunt gave her one then, after a moment, reached for the binoculars and focussed them on the digging site. He caught a brief glimpse of Ryan moving between the office huts, but the site seemed strangely empty of life with only a couple of workmen near the gate.

It puzzled him, but he lowered the glasses and nudged Inez gently.

"We'll start again in a couple of minutes. Work further to the right this time." He grinned encouragingly. "If he's here, we'll find him."

"*Quando* . . . and then what?" she asked almost dispiritedly. "What will happen to him? That's what I kept asking myself back at the house." Her small, white teeth showed in a mirthless smile. "The only answer I had was to go and find those books you wanted."

"The ones Preston gave him?" Gaunt felt a jab of interest. "What are they like?"

"A mixture. Picture books, and one or two infant school readers. Luis was beginning to manage some of the simple words — but he lost his temper when a difficult one beat him."

"Nothing else? More personal, I mean — a scrapbook, a diary, old postcards?"

"No." She shook her head firmly. "Manuel told me all about your Treasure Trove thing, Jonathan. But there was nothing that could help you."

"It doesn't matter." Rolling over on his

back, Gaunt looked up at the lacework of branches. "Right now. I'd settle for just knowing what makes Luis keep coming back here."

"I told you, we often played near the Castelo when we were young." Her lips shaped a momentary smile. "These woods were like magic to us, full of dens and hideaways. I remember when Luis was working for the navy in the valley a few years ago, he took a day off and we came back up here together — a long time had passed, but it still just seemed like the day before."

It took a moment to sink in. Then Gaunt jerked round to face her.

"Say that again."

"About the dens and . . . " Eyes widening, she sat up quickly. "The dens and hideaways, Jonathan! Do you think . . . "

"The other part first," urged Gaunt. "He did a job for the Portuguese navy here?"

She nodded impatiently. "About two years before the accident. They were laying some kind of underground cable and Luis supervised this section because he knew the area."

Gaunt moistened his lips. "A communications cable?"

"Something like that. Though they all wore civilian clothes and tried to pretend they were laying a sewer — it was supposed to be secret."

He swore under his breath. "Can you remember anything more about it, Inez?"

"I think it was a land link between the NATO people at Cape Roca and their headquarters outside Lisbon — some thing like that, anyway." It hardly mattered to her, the new possibility uppermost in her mind. "Jonathan, suppose he went to one of those old dens where we used to play!"

"Wait." Gaunt said it harshly and saw her flinch.

But so much had suddenly begun slotting into place.

Cape Roca — a communications centre probably handling everything from satellite links to nuclear submarine traffic every day of the week. With a constant two-way flow of information along the landline from the Cape to Maritime Headquarters.

If it could be tapped, even for a short length of time, the NATO naval cupboard could be stripped bare of secrets. It was a thought big enough to make him shiver.

Inez was watching him, her eyes puzzled and anxious.

"You're right," he told her soberly. "We'll start trying those hideaways, any you can remember."

Trapped inside his damaged mind, Luis Torres must still have sensed something was wrong in the Castelo valley — something that should matter to him even if he couldn't understand why. And some surviving instinct must have forced him out over these hills night after night on a blind, helpless quest beyond outside comprehension.

Because, like the doctor in Lisbon had admitted, there were things about the human mind, even a damaged human mind, far beyond normal understanding.

Things that projected Luis Torres into a new, personal danger.

He got up, drew Inez back into the deeper shelter of the trees, and checked the pistol in his waistband with a feeling it might be needed now.

"Where do we start?" he asked.

She hesitated, frowned to the right for a moment, then changed her mind and pointed to the left instead.

"That way. It isn't far."

A couple of minutes walking brought them to the first of the Torres family's childhood dens, a mere outcrop of rock forming what imagination might have called a cave. But it was shelter, and someone had been there. Crouching his way in under the ledge, Gaunt brought out the paper-wrapped remains of an old sandwich and some chocolate wrappings. The bread was days old, hard and stale.

"But it means we could be right," said Inez eagerly. "Anna sometimes gives him sandwiches — can we keep trying?"

"We've got to," he said ominously, tossing the finds down. "All right, where next?"

"There's one we called the house den. We both like it, and . . . "

She stopped short, wide-eyed, at the sudden bark of a gun. It came from not far distant then they heard a second shot — this time followed by a shout. For Gaunt, it seemed like a sickeningly familiar echo of where he'd come in.

They headed back to the edge of the woodland at a run then stopped. Down below, a jeep-load of men were driving away from the Castelo diggings. The vehicle was travelling fast, bumping and bouncing its way over the grassland and travelling north up the little valley.

Bringing up the binoculars, Gaunt looked along the route it was taking and understood. A rifle in one hand, waving the jeep on towards him with the other, Carlos Pereira was standing at the edge of the trees about half a kilometre along from them.

"What is it?" asked Inez hoarsely, gripping his arm. "What's happened?"

"My guess is they've spotted him." Gaunt lowered the glasses grimly, knowing they had to gamble now. "If he's running, the odds are he's making for somewhere he feels he can hide — somewhere he thinks of as safety."

"The house den is over there." She bit her lip hard. "It's the only place I can think he'd go."

Gaunt took another glance down at the speeding jeep. Pereira had fired twice. It might have been a signal or it might mean that already Luis Torres was dead or wounded. But one thing was certain — if he was somewhere among those trees and trying to escape he stood little chance on his own.

To try to find him meant heading straight into danger. But if Pereira got there first, Torres' fate was certain. It was very clear now that Luis Torres dead was a factor several people needed to protect their plans.

"Let's move," he said curtly.

And called himself a fool.

8

LEADING the way through the dark woodland, ignoring clawing scrub and barely slowing to dodge the hazards of half-buried tree roots, Inez Torres set a fast, loping pace born from fear and kept going by sheer determination. Keeping up with her slim, fleet-footed figure needed all of Gaunt's energy while his breath became a rasping rhythm and perspiration soaked his body.

He heard no further shots or shouts. But he had no time to think about it as the raven-haired girl continued on her way. When she did finally slow and stop he had lost all sense of distance and direction. But they were at the edge of a tiny gorge carved by a small, dried-up stream.

"There it is," she said, breathless but triumphant, pointing to where an old pine tree lay uprooted like a bridge across the gap. "That's the house den."

Moistening his lips, Gaunt nodded then looked around and listened. He thought he heard a faint shout somewhere, but it was distant, as if the searchers were heading away from them.

He hoped that, anyway.

"Try calling him," he managed hoarsely. "But keep it low."

She called Luis's name softly, waited, then tried again.

Suddenly, there was a rustling movement beneath the fallen tree. A dark head looked out, and with a noise like a sob Inez went scrambling down and began running along the puddled stream.

Gaunt followed her down and arrived beside the fallen tree to find her hugging a haggard, unkempt Luis Torres. Seeing him, Torres made a quick, struggling movement.

"*Nao* . . . no, Luis," said his sister in a quick, soothing voice. "You know Senhor Gaunt. He came to help."

Subsiding, Torres looked at Gaunt again then nodded and grinned weakly. He was wearing an old sweater and slacks, he had shoes, and the one-time play-den beneath the tree held a grubby sleeping bag and an ancient rucksack. Puzzled, Gaunt lifted the rucksack flap, saw the food packed inside, and suddenly understood.

"Jaime," he said wryly. "It couldn't be anyone else."

"Luis, was Jaime here?" asked Inez.

"*Sim.*" The grubby, unshaven scarecrow brightened at the name. "Jaime came."

"Where is he now, Luis?" asked Gaunt with a swift foreboding.

Torres stared at him helplessly and shook his head. Then, without warning, he tried to stand but sank down again with a moan of pain. For the first time Gaunt noticed his left ankle, which had a crude rag bandage tied round it above the shoe.

"He's been hurt." For a moment Inez showed a trace of panic then recovered and knelt down, unwrapping the rag. Badly bruised, Torres' ankle looked swollen to twice normal size but didn't seem broken. She glanced up at Gaunt, dismayed. "What will we do? He can't walk like this . . . "

"We'll manage," Gaunt reassured her. "Try to fix him up the best you can — and ask him what's been happening. I'll be back."

Climbing up to the lip of the little gorge, he stayed there for a full couple of minutes peering out at the surrounding scrub and timber while down below Inez talked softly and drew low, mumbling replies. At last, satisfied the area was still clear, Gaunt slithered down again to join them. "All quiet," he confirmed. "What does he say?"

"He fell this morning, when some men were chasing him." She had soaked the rag bandage in one of the small pools beside them and was busy binding it round her brother's ankle again. "But he hid, then managed to crawl here and — well, Jaime appeared."

"How would Jaime know where to look?"

She shrugged, finishing the task. "He knows Luis and he grew up here too — so he knows these woods." Then, as a new thought struck her, she looked up with a sudden horror. "If it was Jaime they were shooting at . . . "

"He's pretty good at taking care of himself," said Gaunt soberly. "He's also got enough sense to lead them well away from here."

"If he had the chance."

"Jaime makes his own luck." Gaunt eased past her and smiled reassuringly at Torres. "*Para tras* . . . time to go back home. Okay?"

Torres nodded eagerly. Stopping, Gaunt helped him upright, gripped him round his thin waist, and felt Torres clutch at his shoulder for support.

"We'll try it this way," he told Inez. "Let's go."

There was an easy way out of the stream bed not far along. Once they were out, Inez led the way again through the trees while Gaunt assisted Torres a few paces behind. They moved slowly, Inez murmuring an occasional warning as she skirted a rabbit hole or half-concealed root, her brother hopping along with only a few muttered protests.

After a spell they stopped for a brief rest. Torres was breathing hard and, when they started again, Gaunt let him go only a couple of paces then halted and lifted him on his back. Two thin arms clinging round his neck, he nodded to Inez and they moved off.

They made better time that way. Soon the downward slope became steeper and the trees showed a first sign of thinning.

"Not far now," encouraged Inez, glancing back anxiously.

Though he felt like a plodding packhorse, Gaunt managed an answering grin and hefted Torres fractionally higher on his shoulders. Then, as his feet sank into a soft patch of leaf and mould, Gaunt heard Inez give a gasp.

He looked up again — and stopped in mid-stride. Heavy face a carved, scowling mask, Arthur Sollas stood a few yards ahead with a pump-action shotgun held at his hip, the muzzle pointed squarely.

"Stay like that," rasped Sollas. He took two more steps away from the thick clump of scrub which had concealed him then halted and raised his voice. "Pracard!"

The little foxy-faced camp watchman emerged from behind a tree to their right. Similarly armed, he came over grinning with satisfaction and stopped with his gun inches from Gaunt's stomach.

"Put Torres down," ordered Sollas

curtly. "Then move away from him."

Tight-lipped, Gaunt eased Torres from his back, sat him on the ground, then was prodded clear. Shoving him on, Pracard brought him facing a tree, stopped him there, then lowered the shotgun and rapidly checked him over. The automatic and truncheon were found and stuffed into one of the watchman's pockets, then it was Luis Torres' turn.

Torres tried to shrink back as the grinning figure approached him. But Pracard cuffed him hard across the face. repeated the task roughly, then glanced at Sollas and shook his head.

"Make sure of the girl." Sollas's shotgun still hadn't wavered.

Pale-faced and angry, Inez was subjected to the same pawing process then the man stood back. Satisfied, Sollas raised his gun in the air and fired three times. As the spread of pellets brought twigs and leaves raining down from overhead three similarly timed shots answered like an echo from the distance.

"Now what?" asked Gaunt wearily.

"Pick that object up again." Sollas glared in angry contempt at Luis Torres, who cringed like an unhappy schoolboy. "We're going down to Castelo." He sniffed hard and grunted. "Three of you — that's two more than I expected when I said I'd watch this end in case Torres tried to double back. All right, Gaunt, lift him."

"And what happens once we're down there?" Gaunt's half-step forward ended as Pracard's gun jabbed hard against his side.

"What you deserve. Though it wouldn't take much to make me finish it right here," answered Sollas bleakly. "That goes for you in particular, Gaunt. I wouldn't waste time giving you a trial."

Gaunt stared at him, with a sudden, slender hope.

"How much do you really know, Doctor Sollas?" he asked softly.

"Any fool can see it," said Sollas. "Finding you together is the last proof I need. The Marshes are dead, you can get the girl to lodge a claim with your department — and how you planned to split that Treasure Trove money is no concern of mine, damn you."

Inez shook her head desperately. "You

can't believe that. Doctor, we can prove . . . "

"Do you think I'd even listen?" Sollas cut her short with an outraged snarl. "Don't waste your breath. I'd bet you can get that poor damned wreck of a brother to do anything — and Gaunt can probably do the same with you."

She stood white-faced and speechless but Gaunt tried again.

"You're being fooled," he said bitterly. "You're surrounded by men who couldn't care less about your piddling little Roman villa — hell, they knew it was there all along."

"You're a talker all right." Sollas gave a twist of grim admiration then slowly brought the shotgun round until it was trained on Luis Torres. "Well, talk all you want later. But either pick him up — or watch him die."

Gaunt began moving towards Torres then looked back for one last attempt.

"Sollas, there's a NATO communications cable down there. That's what they . . . "

Pracard's gun-barrel cracked him across the side of the face. He staggered, tasted blood in his mouth, and saw the gun raised again. Dazed and shaking his head, he stooped and lifted Torres.

* * *

A few trudging minutes brought them to the edge of the woodland at a spot little more than a stone's throw away from the bulk of the Castelo watchtower. Bernard Ryan's jeep-load of men was on its way back too and skidded to a halt beside their procession as they arrived at the digging site gates.

"Nicely done, Doc!" Jumping down from the driving seat, Ryan came over and greeted Sollas enthusiastically. "All three together — any trouble?"

"None." Sollas rubbed his scarred nose, glanced at Gaunt sardonically, and shook his head. "They walked right into us up there."

"Well, it looks like I was right all along, eh?" The tall, white-haired photographer looked round as the other men from the jeep reached him. "Carlos . . ."

"*Sim*, Senhor Ryan?" Pereira pushed forward, a mocking delight on his pockmarked face as he considered Gaunt.

"Shove them into the hut," ordered Ryan.

"Then call the *policia* at Claras and get them out here," added Sollas grimly. "I want rid of them."

Turning, Pereira gave some quick instructions to his companions — and Gaunt, taking the chance to look around. felt a last hope fade. The whole site area was empty and deserted, there were only the men around them and two more, armed with rifles, waiting by the huts. Perhaps half a dozen in all — before he could check again he was being shoved forward, Torres still clinging bewilderedly to his back and Inez being dragged along beside them.

The one relief when they were inside the hut was that he could drop Luis Torres into the nearest chair. Pereira waved his companions out again then stood covering his three prisoners with a rifle. Too tired to do more than cling to the edge of a workbench, Gaunt watched Inez whisper reassuringly to her brother then pulled himself upright a little as Arthur Sollas came in, followed by Ryan.

"Happy now?" asked Gaunt wryly. "You're still a fool, Sollas."

"You don't give up, do you?" His shotgun crooked under one arm, Sollas gave a snort of contempt.

"Try getting that call through to the police like you wanted," suggested Gaunt caustically. "Go ahead — try."

"What does he mean, Doc?" asked Ryan with an unusual mildness, coming between them.

"They tried to make me swallow a wild story up there — the kind you'd expect." Sollas propped the shotgun against the wall, opened a cupboard, and brought out a whisky bottle. "The general idea was I should let them go."

"What kind of story?" persisted Ryan.

"Wild, as I said." Sollas found a glass and poured himself a drink without looking round. "All about how some of our people must have killed the Marshes. Then some nonsense about the Roman villa and a piece of idiocy about a military cable." The filled glass in his hands, he turned and frowned a little as he saw Pereira hadn't moved. "Carlos, get that call in."

Pereira stayed where he was and raised a faint eyebrow towards Ryan, who shook his head.

"Sorry, Doc," murmured Ryan sadly. "It's not convenient."

A Lüger pistol had appeared in his hand and was trained on Sollas's middle. Sollas froze, staring at it, the glass almost at his lips. Then, open-mouthed in disbelief, he glanced at Pereira and met a lopsided grin.

"We tried to warn you, Doctor." said Inez quietly.

"It sounds like you did," mused Ryan. "But he always was pig-headed. Move, Doc — over beside them."

For a moment Sollas hesitated then he made a snatch for the shotgun. The Lüger barked, its bullet blasting splinters of wood from the stock of the gun and knocking it clear.

"Next time is for real, Doc," said Ryan softly. "Get beside them."

Tight-lipped with fury, Sollas obeyed reluctantly.

"Good." The Lüger swinging from his trigger finger, Ryan perched himself on the edge of the workbench and sighed as he said. "Life gets complicated, that's for sure."

"Like now?" asked Gaunt ironically, flexing his stiffened back muscles and stretching upright. Ignoring Pereira's warning scowl, he brought out his cigarettes and lit one. "I've a feeling the good doctor thinks the same."

"All I feel is that the world is going mad," exploded Sollas. He was still clutching the whisky glass, though most of the contents had slopped down his clothes, and he drained what remained at a single, gulping swallow then abandoned the glass to point a quivering, angry finger at Ryan. "Damn you, I don't care what kind of fraudulent idiocies have been going on. We can talk about that later. But we've got Torres, the police want him for double murder — and maybe these other two as well before they're done."

"Forget it," said Ryan curtly. He eased down from the workbench, came over to where Torres was sitting, and grimaced as the puzzled, dishevelled figure gave him a hopeful smile. Ryan sighed again and looked at Inez.

"Don't think we wanted it this way," he said almost apologetically. "Things just happened, that's all."

The hut door swung open and one of the men from the jeep strode in. Ignoring Sollas, he murmured briefly to Pereira then went out again.

"That's how it is, Doc," nodded Ryan, amused at Sollas's expression. "You okayed me sending most of the squad home for the day — anyone still around is on our side in this."

"And what the hell side is that?" bristled Sollas.

Ryan shrugged. "Ask Gaunt. He seems to know."

Swearing, the big man swung on Gaunt.

"Make some sense out of this," he appealed.

"Go ahead, Gaunt," encouraged Ryan softly. "I'm interested too — things were going smoothly enough until you turned up."

Gaunt looked at the white-haired, oddly smiling figure and knew a lot of things didn't matter any more. Any hopes he had left were slim, and for the rest there was little to lose.

"Including Preston's murder?" he asked, and heard a startled grunt from Sollas. "Preston — then John Marsh and his wife. They were complications too, I suppose."

Ryan's mouth shaped a sudden, hard line. Then, unexpectedly, he shrugged.

"You're guessing — and that disappoints me," he complained, scratching his chin lightly with the Lüger's fore-sight.

The sound of a car drawing up reached them from outside. Hearing it, Ryan gave a faint, reassuring nod to Pereira. Then he considered Gaunt again.

"I'll take a bet you've been guessing most of the way," he declared. "Guessing, with no one else in on the game. Right?"

Suddenly, Inez Torres had had enough. Too fast for anyone to stop her, she reached Ryan and slapped him hard across the mouth. The sound echoed in the hut like an angry whipcrack and Ryan's head jolted back. For a heart-stopping moment his grip tightened on the Lüger — then instead he laughed and shoved her back towards the chair.

"*Obrigado,* sweetheart," he said dryly. "But don't try that again. Once is enough."

"For you?" Raw contempt in her voice, Inez put a sheltering arm around her brother. "You've made people hunt Luis like — like some kind of animal. Does that make you feel proud and clever?"

"I didn't enjoy it, sweetheart." Ryan felt his mouth gingerly, then turned to Gaunt as if he found that easier. "Guessing or not, I'll give you first prize — Preston and the Marshes."

"Preston because he saw too much that night?"

Ryan nodded.

"And the Marshes?"

"Like I said, life gets complicated," said Ryan defensively, ignoring a click behind him as the hut door opened again.

"Very complicated by the look of things," murmured a new voice from the doorway.

Arthur Sollas stared open-mouthed and made a throaty noise of complete disbelief. Jerking round, Gaunt felt the same way as he saw Martin Lawson standing there, the sunlight from outside glinting on his bald head a fluffy halo of hair. Lawson stayed in the doorway a moment more, his expression one of customary mildness. But as he came in and closed the door again there was an unmistakable authority in the way he nodded to Pereira and Ryan.

"We'll talk outside," he said curtly.

"We'd better," agreed Ryan heavily.

With a struggle, Arthur Sollas managed a choked, dazed whisper.

"You, Martin?"

"That's right." Lawson's smile faded as his glance flickered over to Gaunt. "All unexpected, believe me — but I haven't forgotten what happened at our last meeting, Mr Gaunt."

"I was afraid of that," said Gaunt wryly. He dropped his cigarette and stubbed it out under one heel. "But that was when I thought Salvador gave the orders."

"Salvador?" Lawson found the notion amusing. "He makes a good contact man."

300

"When he doesn't over-reach," grunted Ryan.

"Many people do that," murmured Lawson.

He beckoned Ryan and they went out of the hut together. A moment passed, then Pracard and another man, a stolid, dull-faced figure with a shotgun, came in. Pracard carried a length of rope and had Gaunt's F.N. automatic jutting from his waistband and their arrival was the signal for Pereira to leave. The two newcomers began with Gaunt and Sollas, lashing their hands behind their backs. Unemotionally, ignoring his feeble protests, they did the same to Luis Torres then, after completing the same task with Inez, they made all four captives sit on the floor.

Satisfied, Pracard began wandering around the hut examining the site photographs pinned to the walls. His companion relaxed against a filing cabinet, yawning a little.

"Damn them all," said Arthur Sollas in a low, grey voice. "Gaunt, it doesn't help. But I'm sorry."

Gaunt shrugged, more concerned with

testing the rope round his wrists. It was tight and unyielding.

"At least you know what's going on — or some of it," muttered Sollas bitterly. "You could tell me that much."

"And you'd listen now." Inez put a sting behind the words.

Glumly, Sollas nodded.

It was always something to keep their minds off what was being discussed outside. Gaunt talked, keeping his voice low though the men on guard showed no interest. He left out a few details, including Jaime having been in the forest, because it still seemed better that way. Sollas listened intently, and some of it was also new to Inez.

At the finish, Sollas swallowed hard then squirmed round to look at Luis Torres, who was sitting calmly and blank-eyed, as if in some secret world of his own.

"But it all seemed so — so positive." He moistened his lips. "There was that cigarette lighter . . . "

"They'd chased him other times," mused Gaunt. "Maybe they found it, or maybe they took it if they caught him earlier. Then — well, he was getting to be a nuisance and he made a perfect suspect."

Cursing under his breath, Sollas nodded. "And all the time they had me fooled."

"They had Preston fooled too, and he knew plenty of tricks," reminded Gaunt dryly. "But give them credit — they put a lot of work into all this, long-term work. They knew they couldn't just dig down to this NATO cable without being spotted. Instead, they found the other way."

"A full-scale, drum-beating archaeological dig . . . " Sollas sighed his understanding.

"Great big trenches all over the place and a lot of unofficial overtime," agreed Gaunt. "Now you know why the Portuguese were so edgy about permissions — even when you and Preston were being used as a high-class front."

"Does any of it matter now?" asked Inez in a low voice. "Jonathan, they're going to kill us, aren't they?"

The door opening again saved him from having to answer. Martin Lawson came in alone and stood over them, frowning a little and sucking his teeth.

"We've found where the girl hid her car," he said suddenly. "I'm going along with Ryan on the rest — that you were in this on your own and that there's no risk of anyone missing you for a few hours. That's all we need." Coming closer, he prodded Gaunt with a foot. "Get up — that goes for all of you. I'm putting you somewhere else for now."

"Then what?" asked Gaunt bluntly.

"Get up," said Lawson without answering.

"*Por Favor* . . . " Inez spoke wearily. "My brother will need help. He — his ankle is hurt."

"Look for yourself," growled Sollas. "Any fool can see that's true."

"A medical opinion, too?" Lawson gave him a watery smile. "The girl can help."

He gave an order to Pracard, who produced a knife and cut Inez and Torres loose. Then, pushed and prodded to their feet, Inez half-supporting her brother, they were bundled out of the hut and hustled past the excavation trenches towards the ruin of the Castelo tower. Ryan and Pereira were there, standing

304

beside the archway.

"Opened up?" asked Lawson.

Pereira nodded.

"Ryan and I will cope here," Lawson told him. "You stay around the huts in case of visitors."

Obediently, Pereira strode off while Ryan led the way through the archway into the dank, shadowed gloom of the old tower. Gaunt and the others were pushed along after him, squeezing past blocks of fallen masonry and into a short, narrow passage which led to a small inner room. Two of the slabs of its flagstone floor had been removed and a bright glow of light came up from below.

"Down there," said Ryan briefly, gesturing to the top rungs of a sloping iron ladder.

"With our hands tied?" queried Sollas in disgust. "We could break our necks."

"You worry me," said Ryan cynically. He nodded to Pracard, who grinned and disappeared down the rungs. Then he beckoned Gaunt. "You first."

Keeping his back to the sloping ladder, Gaunt managed to get down about a dozen rungs before he missed his footing.

He bumped and slid the rest of the way, to land with a thud on another stone floor only a few more feet down. Sollas was less lucky, tumbling after he'd hardly started and crashing down. He was still groaning with pain as he was kicked back on his feet.

Lawson climbed down next then, as the others followed, Gaunt found himself being pushed on again through a low, narrow tunnel built of old, rough stonework but with new electric lights wired along one side at intervals. He had to stop to get through, while cobwebs brushed his face and large spiders scurried to escape into crannies in the stone. Here and there, he saw places where cement patches repaired gaps in the original structure.

"It dates back to Roman times," said Lawson suddenly, crouching along behind him. "This was the villa's water culvert — they tapped a stream from the hill." He kept on in the same almost conversational voice, as if he was lecturing to a favoured student. "From here it went to a cistern in the villa, then they drew it off as required. The — ah — Moors used it later, but only as a form of sewer. Still, they were clever people too."

"And the rest was all your own idea?" Gaunt swore as a low projection grazed his head.

"That's right," agreed Lawson modestly. "I counted on something like it — and it saved a lot of work, believe me." He sighed a little. "We weren't so fortunate beyond the villa. I'd hoped for a drainage culvert — but we hit nothing but inferior clay piping, most of it broken."

"Maybe the Romans ran out of pennies," suggested Gaunt sourly.

"That's possible," Lawson mused on the notion for a moment. "Yes, you could be right. It's a pity we can't talk about it more — I really mean that."

They had reached the end of the tunnel, or more exactly the lip where it fell away into what had once been the Roman villa's vast underground cistern. Stone walls and a smooth stone floor were lit by more electric bulbs, and Lawson pushed him on down a new ramp of earth into the middle.

Able to stand upright again and left alone for a moment as the others stumbled down, he looked around quickly and felt a reluctant admiration for what had been done.

The old cistern was saucer-shaped, about twenty feet across, and perhaps half as high as it was broad. On one side the original Roman-built wall had been hacked away to form a smaller chamber which held a litter of shovels, timber props and other equipment. Beside it, the black mouth of a low, new, and much smaller tunnel than the one they'd come through had two thin cables trailing out to link to a trio of small, grey-finished metal cabinets. A small diesel generator stood beside them, linked to a bank of lead-acid batteries, its exhaust pipe a flexible tube snaking back into the main tunnel.

"Look, but don't touch," said Bernard Ryan sardonically, blocking his way as he took a tentative step nearer the cabinets. He thumbed to where Pracard and the other guard were herding Inez, Sollas and a surprisingly calm Luis Torres against the opposite wall. "That's your side of the fence."

"Let him stay," murmured Lawson,

with a chilly benevolence. "Ryan's sensitive about his equipment, Gaunt. But one could say you've earned this much."

"A last favour before a carbon copy of the Marsh business?" asked Gaunt bleakly. "Four of us will take a lot of explaining."

Ryan winced, but stayed silent, glancing at Lawson.

"That disgusted me — but was necessary," declared Lawson slowly. "We . . . " He stopped and shook his head. "Leave it. Gaunt, I am a professional, and my masters in Moscow dislike unnecessary violence as much as I do, even if for slightly different reasons. But sometimes there is no option. The Marshes, for instance" — his mouth tightened — "an objectionable couple, for a start. They were caught inside the office hut, after breaking into Ryan's desk. Obviously they were hoping some of their uncle's papers might be hidden inside. Instead, they found some" — he glared at Ryan — "some unfortunate drawings and paperwork which should not have been there."

"So they were killed, and you framed Luis Torres."

"We had a lot to lose," shrugged Lawson. "We've been through to the NATO cable for almost two weeks. Monitoring its signal impulses is no great technical problem, and analysing the tapes isn't our concern. We simply pass them on. But this is a long-term project — no here today, gone tomorrow affair."

Abruptly, he went over to the bank of equipment, quickly flicking switches and not looking back.

"Talking's over — back with the rest of them," ordered Ryan quickly, gesturing with the Lüger. He twisted a humourless grin. "I've work to do. Cape Roca has a computer feed chatter with Lisbon due in about ten minutes — it's becoming one of our regular tapings."

The equipment bank was coming to life as Ryan herded him over to where Inez, Torres and Arthur Sollas were already squatting on the stone floor under Pracard's sharp-eyed supervision. Ryan beckoned Pracard's thick-set companion, who slouched over casually nursing the shotgun in his grasp.

"*Quero* . . . I want this one watched," warned Ryan.

"*Sim.*" The man grinned and shoved Gaunt down next to Inez.

Leaving them, Ryan went back to join Lawson at the recording equipment. Gaunt tried to wriggle into a more comfortable position, found having his hands tied behind him made it difficult, then he felt Inez helping him.

"Thanks." He grimaced wryly and looked around. Arthur Sollas was still tied and met his gaze with a gloomy scowl, but so far no one seemed to have bothered about Inez or her brother.

"Did they say what will happen?" asked Inez quietly.

"I don't think they know themselves," he lied. "How's Luis?"

"Happy," she said oddly but meant it.

Luis was sitting staring at the equipment bank, almost drinking in its murmur of sound. At that moment, a high-pitched tone howl as Ryan adjusted a control brought a smile to his haggard, unshaven young face and his lips began moving, silently shaping words to himself.

It was as if some long-buried memories were being stirred awake, their plight a completely obscured irrelevancy.

In a few minutes the recording gear was ready enough to satisfy Lawson. He left Ryan, crossed the cistern floor, and spoke for a moment to Pracard. Then he frowned down at Inez.

"Tie her hands again — the same with her brother," he ordered, and switched his attention to Gaunt. "You'll be here for a spell. I wouldn't try any heroics — that would be fairly senseless."

Without waiting for an answer he turned and went away, going up the earth ramp and into the culvert tunnel towards the Castelo tower.

Ryan was still working at the recording gear as Pracard began wandering around, poking at the digging equipment and looking for something to use as rope. He found a section of cut cable, frowned down at it, then changed his mind and was starting to search again when Ryan called him over.

"Can't we do anything?" muttered Sollas, watching the two men moving one of the recording units and Ryan making adjustments to some hidden control at the rear.

"Like what?" Gaunt looked up wistfully at the remaining guard. "Shall I bite his ankle and hope he bleeds to death?"

Sollas glared and faced away, muttering to himself. After a moment, Gaunt eased closer to Inez then casually turned to screen her from view, nudging with his hands. She understood, shifted her own position with a deliberate sigh — then, seconds later, her fingers were working on the tightly knotted rope at his wrists.

Suddenly, the man on guard stopped being sleepy-eyed. He shoved forward, kicked Gaunt angrily on the side, and forced Inez over until she was beside Luis.

"Next time . . ." He scowled and gestured with the butt of his shotgun.

At last, Ryan had finished with the recording unit. He had Pracard help him shove it back, checked the result with another warbling tone note which echoed round the stone walls, and was ready. Glancing at his wristwatch, he grinned coldly across at Gaunt.

"They're finishing their coffee-break at Cape Roca. Those computer operators stick to routine. They'll be making their own line-checks in a minute or two."

A flick of a switch brought a pale glow of lights along the smaller tunnel. Going over to it, Ryan went down on all fours and disappeared inside.

Whistling thinly through his teeth, Gaunt tried to calculate how long the tunnel might go. From the middle of the Roman villa, probably, to somewhere in the open ground outside the site fence. Maybe a hundred yards, a reasonable construction job on its own. At the other end, once they'd reached the cable, he expected installing the monitoring 'bug' equipment had been simple by comparison — a question of skill, just as deciphering the signals it captured and taped was something for other skills.

And he couldn't do a damned thing about any of it.

He sighed as the soft tone from the recording gear switched to a new, broken rhythm. Then, suddenly, he noticed Luis Torres.

As the new rhythm warbled on, Torres

frowned, looked puzzled, and before Inez could stop him was on his feet, holding to the wall for support and hobbling nearer. Pracard saw him, nudged the other guard, and grinned, watching but doing nothing.

Slowly, Torres came nearer to the recording banks. His face was twisted in concentration, Inez was staring at him in bewilderment — and Gaunt winced, sensing what was coming a moment before it happened.

Strolling over, Pracard stuck out a foot and tripped him. The other guard came over, gave a coarse laugh at the way Torres lay sprawled, and deliberately hit him in the stomach with the shotgun butt. As Torres gave a retch of agony the heavy butt swung back again, this time aiming for his head.

The blow didn't land. Inez Torres was there first, throwing herself bodily at the thick-set figure, nails scratching raw furrows down his face as she clawed for his eyes. Cursing, her opponent tried to fend her off while Pracard joined in, seizing her by the hair and trying to wrench her away. Both men were cursing, Arthur Sollas was struggling upright, Gaunt was trying to do the same — and for the moment Luis Torres was forgotten.

Suddenly, Inez gave a cry of pain as the thick-set man twisted her arm viciously. Up at last, Gaunt started forward — then stopped, mesmerised.

Luis Torres was also up again, somehow staying on his feet, a twisted, determined fury in his thin face — and a metal crowbar in his hands. He took two swaying, hobbling steps forward, balanced on his good ankle, and smashed the bar down with both hands on the thick-set man's skull.

The thud of the blow blended with the louder noise as the guard tumbled limp, the shotgun clattering. Inez stumbled back while Pracard spun, grabbing the automatic from his waistband.

He triggered twice at the thin, swaying figure before him and Luis Torres fell, his mouth opened wide in a soundless surprise. Snarling, Pracard brought the automatic round again aiming for Inez — but the bullet went wide as Gaunt body-charged him back against the wall and the next moment Sollas was there too, hurling his massive weight in a bull-like desperation which threw Pracard down on the stone floor.

The automatic was still in Pracard's fist, and he was wriggling clear. Gaunt kicked, took Pracard hard on the wrist, and the weapon went skidding across the floor to stop near Inez. She stared at it, then, as Gaunt shouted, picked it up.

Pracard scrambled to his feet, saw her, and made a dive towards the fallen shotgun. She pulled the trigger three times, and he screamed once, jerked, and died with his fingers still scrabbling.

The echo of the shots faded and, for a moment, there was only the monotonous warbling of the recording banks. Arthur Sollas was sitting back against the stonework, breathing heavily and with blood staining his left shoulder. Inez hadn't moved, the automatic held limp at her side, her face the colour of parchment . . . and her brother still lay as he had fallen. But there was still Ryan in the cable tunnel. Gaunt moistened his lips.

"Pracard had a knife," he said urgently. "Get it, Inez."

She looked round slowly, her eyes blank.

"The knife, Inez," he insisted. "Get it."

It sank in. Listlessly, she found the knife, brought it over, and cut the rope from his wrists. Wincing at the first return of circulation, Gaunt took the knife over to Arthur Sollas, cut him free, and looked round again.

Inez was down on her knees beside her brother, sobbing quietly. Gaunt went to her, removed the gun gently from her hand then turned and saw the lights in the cable tunnel had gone out. He reached its entrance at a run, flopped down beside it — and a shot slammed out at him, the bullet ricochetting wildly off the stonework above his head.

Bringing the automatic up, he fired once in a blind reply and heard a startled, muffled curse.

"Ryan" — he raised his voice in a shout, but kept clear of the tunnel mouth, a perfect target frame — "we've taken over at this end. You can come out, but throw that gun out first."

There was silence for several seconds,

then Ryan bellowed back.

"Like hell — and try coming in, Gaunt. I'll sit this one out till you're taken care of from up top."

Another shot from the darkness slammed the stonework in emphasis and Gaunt gave up, looking round as Arthur Sollas crawled beside him, tight-lipped and bringing the shotgun.

"Torres is dead," said Sollas grimly. "Pracard the same — the other one's name was Martinez, and he won't trouble anyone." He propped himself beside Gaunt, sighed, and thumbed back. "The girl's in the next best thing to shock, so don't expect much help there."

"What about you?"

"A nice clean shoulder wound — Pracard's third shot, the one that missed Inez." Sollas grunted almost amiably and hefted the shotgun. "That's the least of my worries right now. How about using this?"

"Just watch him for me," said Gaunt.

Easing back, he went over to Inez. She had stopped sobbing but was still kneeling beside her brother, and when she looked up her face held its own silent agony.

"He's dead," she said simply.

Gently, Gaunt coaxed her to her feet and over beside the recording equipment. He stopped long enough to find a switch that shut off the monotonous chattering tone then went back, took off his jacket and carefully covered Luis Torres' face.

Stepping back, he chewed his lip thoughtfully. Despite the echoing din of these shots, there was every chance nothing had been heard above ground. But Ryan, stuck like a mole in his tunnel, was still right. Any moment might bring someone down from the Castelo — and when that happened there could only be one bloody result.

Yet he had to be sure of Ryan first . . . looking round again, he suddenly saw that part of the answer in the little diesel generator and the cans of fuel which lay beside it.

The generator was on a wheeled trolley, it took only seconds to use the knife to cut its output terminals, and a minute more to slash through the snaking exhaust pipe a few feet from its source. Pracard's body was in the way. He dragged it clear, then wheeled the generator over to be greeted by a frown from Sollas.

"What the hell?" Suddenly, Sollas's expression changed and an appreciative grin twisted across his scarred face. "It should work, but it takes time."

"Maybe he doesn't know that. Keep an eye on the Castelo side for me." Carefully, Gaunt fed the exhaust tube's length down into the tunnel. It slithered along, with enough noise to bring a shot from Ryan, then again there was silence.

"Ryan, listen for a moment," shouted Gaunt. The engine had a simple pull-cord starter and burst into noisy life at the second pull. He gave it full throttle for a few seconds then shut it off again. "Do you know what that was?"

"Don't play games," came a snarled reply from somewhere in the tunnel.

"Remember your science?" called Gaunt. "Exhaust fumes equal carbon monoxide — colourless, odourless, taste-less, but it kills. Symptoms start with shortage of breath and giddiness, then your heart starts racing before you pass out." He crossed his fingers. "Five minutes at most and you're dead."

He heard a curse and two shots whined off the stonework.

"Throw the gun out when you're ready." Gaunt started the little engine again and sent it racing.

A full minute passed then he heard a muffled shout above the throbbing beat. Grinning at Sollas, he closed down the engine and Ryan's automatic came skidding out of the tunnel.

Sullen and grimy, Bernard Ryan followed it out. He emerged coughing and spluttering, looked nervously at the dead men on the floor, doubled in another bout of coughing, then allowed himself to be frisked without uttering a protest.

"Inez, help me." Gaunt gave a faint smile of reassurance as she came over slowly, then handed her Ryan's gun. "Keep him covered."

Silently, she trained the Lüger on Ryan's middle and it stayed like that, unwavering, while Gaunt used a length of electrical wiring to secure the man's hands.

"You still haven't a hope," said Ryan cautiously as he finished.

"That's part of your worry now," Gaunt told him softly. "How many men has Lawson up there?"

Ryan shrugged, growing more confident. "Another four, not counting Pereira. Long odds, friend — unless we maybe do some kind of a deal."

"See that gun Inez is holding?" said Gaunt stonily. "Her brother is dead, Ryan. The only deal left is that maybe you get out of here alive."

Thin face growing paler, Ryan saw the hate in Inez's eyes and cringed back a little.

"I didn't kill anyone," he said urgently, sweat suddenly beading his forehead. "That was all Pereira — he did for Preston."

"What about the Marshes," rasped Sollas from the background.

"The Marshes, too," agreed Ryan hoarsely. "I drove the car the last stage, that's all. Pereira did the rest, Marsh first then the woman." He licked his lips. "It was Pereira's idea to make it look like Torres did it too. He had

323

that cigarette lighter — Torres dropped it one night when we chased him off."

"And you just drove the car." Gaunt considered him with an open contempt. "Congratulations."

Arthur Sollas came over and pushed Ryan back with unconcealed relish. Turning away, Gaunt checked the F.N. automatic which had been Luis Torres' and saw it had six rounds of its thirteen-round magazine remaining. There were four rounds left in the Lüger when he took it from Inez, but he shook his head and returned it.

"I'll come too," she said, reading his mind "I — *por favor*, Jonathan. I don't want to stay here."

He frowned. "Sollas?"

"Another hunk of flex round this character's legs and he wouldn't go far," rumbled Sollas, glaring at Ryan. "Though a bullet would be quicker."

Ryan stared at them, naked fear in his face. "Gaunt . . . "

"Flex," said Gaunt. Then he touched Inez gently on the cheek and nodded. "We'll all go."

They left Ryan bound hand and foot

and started back along the old culvert tunnel which led to the Castelo, Gaunt in the lead with Inez and Sollas close behind.

On the way, Gaunt noticed details he'd missed before. Another time, and he'd have asked Arthur Sollas about some of them, like the apparently perfect blocks of carved masonry lumped in at intervals with the rest of the culvert material because of some probable tiny flaw. He saw other blocks with crudely scratched lettering which might have been the Roman equivalent of graffiti and, strangest, a few broken sections of an oddly veined white marble, worn by surface time but still showing a separate, more delicate carving which had to be from an even earlier age.

Another time . . . what mattered more was his first glimpse of the iron rung ladder which led up to the Castelo.

They were almost there when, unexpectedly, the stone slab hatch above began to grate open. He signalled Sollas and Inez back against the tunnel walls and waited while the slabs were dragged clear and a figure began hastily clambering down.

The man's back was to them. Cat-footing forward, Gaunt could hear him breathing heavily on the last few rungs. Then, as the stranger reached the bottom, Gaunt tapped him lightly on the shoulder.

Yelping in surprise, the man tried to turn — and Gaunt slammed him over the head with the butt of the F.N. pistol, catching him as he fell.

Leaving the unconscious figure to Sollas, he swarmed up the iron ladder with the F.N. ready. But the Castelo room above was empty and the only sound a faint murmur of wind.

Climbing out, he looked back and saw Sollas busy binding and gagging the man with his own tie and belt. He let him finish then signalled them up.

Inez came first and gave him a shaky smile as he helped her out. Sollas was slower, his shoulder troubling him and the slung shotgun bumping, but there was still a triumphant grin on his face as he sat with his legs still dangling over the edge of the hatch.

"That's it," declared Sollas cheerfully.

"Hell, we could fight our own little war from this place."

Gaunt nodded and gave Sollas a minute more to recover before he gestured them on again. Quietly, they made their way back along the rubble-strewn passage to the Castelo door, the bright glow of sunlight pouring in from outside a welcome on its own.

But at its edge Gaunt stopped and stared in sheer disbelief. Down below, a police car was stopped beside the site huts. A couple of uniformed police lounged beside it and Sergeant Costa was strolling casually towards the excavation trenches with Lawson by his side.

Pressing past him in the archway, Arthur Sollas gasped then drew in a deep breath, ready to yell. Gaunt stopped him in time, looked again, and saw that three of Lawson's men were clustered in a tight knot close by the car.

Even if Ryan had been right when he talked, that still left Pereira — and Pereira was the most dangerous.

"Stay here," he said quietly. "I'm going down."

Inez looked at him blankly but Sollas

327

gave a frown which showed he understood and looked wryly at the shotgun.

"There's no real range with this thing," he warned.

Gaunt nodded, checked the F.N. again, then stepped out into the open.

Nobody noticed him at first and he walked quietly down the slope, taking a line to intercept Sergeant Costa and Lawson. Then, about halfway down, he heard a warning shout from the men at the huts, saw Costa turn, stare, reach for his holster — and Carlos Pereira step into view from behind one of the spoil-heaps, a rifle coming up to his shoulder.

Gaunt threw himself sideways, triggering the F.N. as the rifle barked. Pereira's bullet whined close over his head — then the echo of their shots was drowned by the staccato, cyclic rasp of a machine-pistol.

It came from the police car, a long, hosing burst of fire which sent Pereira jerking and twisting like a maddened doll. As it ended, he sank slowly to his knees then collapsed in the dirt.

Then it was quiet, and Gaunt rose slowly. The uniformed men by the police car were no longer lounging and Lawson's trio had their hands in the air. A third officer was climbing out of the car, the machine-pistol in his hands — and the car was going to need a new windscreen.

He walked down to where Pereira lay, saw he was dead, and went straight on to where Manuel Costa was waiting with Lawson. Costa had a revolver in his right hand, covering Martin Lawson, but Lawson still managed a sad, wry smile.

"The others?" asked Costa without preamble as Gaunt reached them.

"Inez and Sollas are all right," said Gaunt, his eyes on Lawson.

"And Luis?"

"Dead." More cars were driving into the camp, filled with police. He watched them for a moment, puzzled, as they stopped and their crews poured out. "How the hell did you know?"

"Jaime," said Costa with a wry pride. "He came with a crazy story about being chased and hiding, then seeing you and Inez and Luis . . . " he stopped and shrugged his slim shoulders. "So I — ah — took certain precautions before I came."

"But you wouldn't have found them," said Lawson, a bitter, weary figure who seemed suddenly aged and drained. Lips tightening, he looked around him. "What happened, Gaunt?"

"Some luck — and Luis Torres," said Gaunt grimly. "Mainly Luis Torres."

Lawson shook his head in near disbelief. "I told you I was a professional, Gaunt," he said hoarsely. "A few more years and my masters had agreed I should retire. It may amuse you. There would even have been a pension. But now . . . "

"We call it *fado*," said Manuel Costa unemotionally. "Fate is something no one can forecast." Then he brightened as he saw Inez coming down from the Castelo with Arthur Sollas close behind her. "My men will take care of the rest here, Senhor Gaunt — I want to be with you when you meet a certain headquarters captain."

"And Jaime," reminded Gaunt.

Costa nodded wryly. "My little black sheep relative, whom I may have to throw in jail some day." He saw Gaunt's raised eyebrow and nodded. "My nephew — you hired his father's car."

Gaunt managed a grin, then went to meet the slim, proud girl coming towards them.

★ ★ ★

Two days later they buried Lieutenant Luis Torres with full naval honours in the little cemetery outside Claras.

Inez was there in black mourning, Gaunt on her one side and Manuel Costa on the other. But an embassy car from Lisbon was waiting by the cemetery gate as the service ended and two hours later Gaunt was on a *Transportes Aeros Portugueses* flight out of Lisbon for London.

It was the middle of the following morning, a grey day of gentle rain in Edinburgh, when he walked into Henry Falconer's room in the Queen's and Lord Treasurer's Remembrancer's office in George Street.

Falconer was behind his desk, looking out at the misting wet with a resigned gloom. He turned and greeted Gaunt with no particular enthusiasm.

"Lisbon sent us a full telex," said Falconer

in his gloomiest Senior Administrative Assistant voice. "You had a busy time."

"It shaped that way," agreed Gaunt carefully.

"Quite." Falconer built a small steeple with his fingertips. "But the Treasure Trove inquiry . . . ?"

"Nothing." Gaunt shook his head.

"So it died with him. A pity." Falconer frowned and unlocked a drawer of his desk. "I — ah — didn't show you this before. Francis Preston gave it to the Remembrancer as — well, he called it a token."

He laid a small, exquisitely shaped silver chalice cup on his desk top and touched it carefully with one finger. "The experts say early Celtic Christian. If the rest was like this — well, we'll just have to hope they turn up some day."

Some day or maybe never. Gaunt looked at it for a moment then reached into the briefcase at his side.

"Yours," he said briefly, placing a bottle of vintage port beside the glinting chalice.

"You remembered — excellent!"

Falconer brightened. "The true wine of the country, eh?"

Gaunt nodded. He'd bought the bottle that morning in a shop along Princes Street.

He could afford that much. The financial pages were leading with the story of a surprise European bid for Consolidated Breweries, which had made an overnight rise of twenty points. The price for Malters shares had crashed.

There was another bottle in his briefcase, for a little old lady out in Morningside.

But he'd be drinking alone.

Which meant thinking of Inez. Though he knew he now stood for too many memories of a kind she wanted to forget.

Fado . . . Manuel Costa had been right when he'd talked about fate.

"Yes, I'll look forward to this," said Falconer, examining the bottle again. "In fact, we could sample it now, eh?"

Gaunt grinned, considered the glinting chalice for a moment, then went for some paper cups.

THE WILDERNESS WALK
Sheila Bishop

Stifling unpleasant memories of a misbegotten romance in Cleave with Lord Francis Aubrey, Lavinia goes on holiday there with her sister. The two women are thrust into a romantic intrigue involving none other than Lord Francis.

THE RELUCTANT GUEST
Rosalind Brett

Ann Calvert went to spend a month on a South African farm with Theo Borland and his sister. They both proved to be different from her first idea of them, and there was Storr Peterson — the most disturbing man she had ever met.

ONE ENCHANTED SUMMER
Anne Tedlock Brooks

A tale of mystery and romance and a girl who found both during one enchanted summer.

CLOUD OVER MALVERTON
Nancy Buckingham

Dulcie soon realises that something is seriously wrong at Malverton, and when violence strikes she is horrified to find herself under suspicion of murder.

AFTER THOUGHTS
Max Bygraves

The Cockney entertainer tells stories of his East End childhood, of his RAF days, and his post-war showbusiness successes and friendships with fellow comedians.

MOONLIGHT
AND MARCH ROSES
D. Y. Cameron

Lynn's search to trace a missing girl takes her to Spain, where she meets Clive Hendon. While untangling the situation, she untangles her emotions and decides on her own future.

NURSE ALICE IN LOVE
Theresa Charles

Accepting the post of nurse to little Fernie Sherrod, Alice Everton could not guess at the romance, suspense and danger which lay ahead at the Sherrod's isolated estate.

POIROT INVESTIGATES
Agatha Christie

Two things bind these eleven stories together — the brilliance and uncanny skill of the diminutive Belgian detective, and the stupidity of his Watson-like partner, Captain Hastings.

LET LOOSE THE TIGERS
Josephine Cox

Queenie promised to find the long-lost son of the frail, elderly murderess, Hannah Jason. But her enquiries threatened to unlock the cage where crucial secrets had long been held captive.

THE TWILIGHT MAN
Frank Gruber

Jim Rand lives alone in the California desert awaiting death. Into his hermit existence comes a teenage girl who blows both his past and his brief future wide open.

DOG IN THE DARK
Gerald Hammond

Jim Cunningham breeds and trains gun dogs, and his antagonism towards the devotees of show spaniels earns him many enemies. So when one of them is found murdered, the police are on his doorstep within hours.

THE RED KNIGHT
Geoffrey Moxon

When he finds himself a pawn on the chessboard of international espionage with his family in constant danger, Guy Trent becomes embroiled in moves and countermoves which may mean life or death for Western scientists.

TIGER TIGER
Frank Ryan

A young man involved in drugs is found murdered. This is the first event which will draw Detective Inspector Sandy Woodings into a whirlpool of murder and deceit.

CAROLINE MINUSCULE
Andrew Taylor

Caroline Minuscule, a medieval script, is the first clue to the whereabouts of a cache of diamonds. The search becomes a deadly kind of fairy story in which several murders have an other-worldly quality.

LONG CHAIN OF DEATH
Sarah Wolf

During the Second World War four American teenagers from the same town join the Army together. Forty-two years later, the son of one of the soldiers realises that someone is systematically wiping out the families of the four men.

THE LISTERDALE MYSTERY
Agatha Christie

Twelve short stories ranging from the light-hearted to the macabre, diverse mysteries ingeniously and plausibly contrived and convincingly unravelled.

TO BE LOVED
Lynne Collins

Andrew married the woman he had always loved despite the knowledge that Sarah married him for reasons of her own. So much heartache could have been avoided if only he had known how vital it was to be loved.

ACCUSED NURSE
Jane Converse

Paula found herself accused of a crime which could cost her her job, her nurse's reputation, and even the man she loved, unless the truth came to light.

BUTTERFLY MONTANE
Dorothy Cork

Parma had come to New Guinea to marry Alec Rivers, but she found him completely disinterested and that overbearing Pierce Adams getting entirely the wrong idea about her.

HONOURABLE FRIENDS
Janet Daley

Priscilla Burford is happily married when she meets Junior Environment Minister Alistair Thurston. Inevitably, sexual obsession and political necessity collide.

WANDERING MINSTRELS
Mary Delorme

Stella Wade's career as a concert pianist might have been ruined by the rudeness of a famous conductor, so it seemed to her agent and benefactor. Even Sir Nicholas fails to see the possibilities when John Tallis falls deeply in love with Stella.

MORNING IS BREAKING
Lesley Denny

The growing frenzy of war catapults Diane Clements into a clandestine marriage and separation with a German refugee.

LAST BUS TO WOODSTOCK
Colin Dexter

A girl's body is discovered huddled in the courtyard of a Woodstock pub, and Detective Chief Inspector Morse and Sergeant Lewis are hunting a rapist and a murderer.

THE STUBBORN TIDE
Anne Durham

Everyone advised Carol not to grieve so excessively over her cousin's death. She might have followed their advice if the man she loved thought that way about her, but another girl came first in his affections.